THE HEART'S RETURN

Painful memories surface when Megan Moore receives an urgent request from Jordan Alexander, at her agency Time Savers. Jordan, having purchased Megan's old family home, wants the property to be made ready for him to move in by the end of the month. Despite her knowing the work would prove an emotional minefield, Megan's interest in Jordan, and the chance of seeing her old home again, are both irresistible. Can she lay her memories to rest and find happiness again?

DOROTHY TAYLOR

THE HEART'S RETURN

Complete and Unabridged

LINFORD
Leicester

First published in Great Britain in 2007

First Linford Edition
published 2008

British Library CIP Data

Taylor, Dorothy
    The heart's return.—Large print ed.—
Linford romance library
    1. Women interior decorators—Fiction
    2. Love stories 3. Large type books
    I. Title
    823.9'14 [F]

ISBN 978–1–84782–298–7

Published by
F. A. Thorpe (Publishing)
Anstey, Leicestershire

Set by Words & Graphics Ltd.
Anstey, Leicestershire
Printed and bound in Great Britain by
T. J. International Ltd., Padstow, Cornwall

This book is printed on acid-free paper

1

Jordan Alexander slammed down his pen and depressed the plastic button on the intercom connecting his office with his secretary's.

'Diane?' He raked his dark hair abstractedly, his brow knotted with concentration. 'The agency that Oliver has been praising to the hilt lately. What was it called? Time something or other?'

'Time Savers,' Diane came back swiftly. 'I suggested they might be able to help with your move. Remember?'

Jordan grimaced. Five years with the firm; three as his secretary, Diane knew him better than he knew himself. 'That's the one. Why don't I listen to you?'

'You tell me,' Diane chuckled. 'Although,' she sobered, 'you must have other things on your mind at the moment.'

'You could say that.' Jordan's grey eyes darkened momentarily then he got back on track. 'Find out what you can about them.'

Jordan leaned back in his chair with a heavy sigh. Unable to settle, he swivelled it around to face the window then got to his feet. Time for a break, he decided. He'd been too long at his desk writing up instructions for the brief that Oliver would be taking over for him during his leave.

He walked across the room and looked out at the familiar scene he'd always felt affection for. Beyond the bustling commercial centre of the city, he could see the Liverpool waterfront, dominated by the three imperial looking buildings, known affectionately as the Three Graces.

Atop the centre building the two eighteen foot high, copper Liver Birds squatted, wings half flapping. One facing towards the river and the other inland gazing over the city. Today, he reflected, the buildings' impressive pale grey construction looked a cool contrast against the brightness of the July sun and vivid blue sky.

He would miss this view for the next six weeks, he realised. But then deep inside him something close to excitement stirred. The time was coming to put the past well and truly behind him as he settled Abbie and himself into a new way of life.

His expression hardened as unwanted memories returned to haunt him. The initial numbing disbelief when first learning of Claire's accident, coupled with his inability to accept no blame for what had happened.

Then the gradual release and an acceptance of what he now expected of life. His mouth hardened.

And the resolve to see it through.

In less than two weeks time a major part of that resolve would finally be materialising. It had to work out.

With the second anniversary of Claire's death coming up, the promise of what this new home held, he fervently hoped, would prove something of a distraction for Abbie.

Wondering not for the first time, how much she remembered of the events leading up to the loss of her mother, he experienced the usual stab of concern. Hopefully, he reflected, very little.

With fresh determination, he walked back to his desk and sat down. His features softened as he looked at the framed photograph in pride of place next to the intercom. His mirror image, he'd been told often enough, in glowing feminine miniature.

The hint of shyness in Abbie's latest school photograph couldn't mask her bubbly personality that, thankfully, was shining through more often these days.

As he regarded his daughter, he became more pensive. She was growing fast. The familiar worry about the lack of a woman's guidance and company for her returned to trouble him. She deserved more than his continuing reliance on her best friend's mother, he contemplated, however willingly Tricia gave it. But what alternative did he have at the moment . . . if ever?

Pushing his concerns to one side, he picked up his pen to begin writing again, but his mind refused to stay focused.

Their move out of their waterfront apartment was the right one. He had no doubts about that. But as a single father of one child, who was determined to remain single, how had he come to buy a country house that could accommodate a football team?

The buzz of the intercom interrupted his thoughts. He pressed the plastic button once more. 'That didn't take long.'

Diane got straight to the point. 'It's a youngish company, so there's not a huge amount of information available on them. But what I do have appears to bear out all Oliver's praise.'

'Sounds good.'

'I think so,' Diane agreed. 'I'm printing out the details so I'll bring them through in a minute. Then you can make up your mind.'

He'd go for it. He had no choice. 'Already done. I've wasted enough time already. If you'll put a call through for me now, I'll read the paperwork later.'

As Jordan cut the connection he grimaced. If he was as organised in his personal life as he was in the partnership, he'd have had this move planned down to the last detail weeks ago.

Instead all he had to show was a few half-filled cardboard boxes and a promised donation to a charity organisation.

His frown deepened. There was no getting away from it. He needed help and he needed it now.

★   ★   ★

'Yes, Jane?' Megan Moore answered the internal phone abstractedly. Her head still full of details in front of her.

'I've a Mr Jordan Alexander on the line. Insists on speaking to you. Won't take no for an answer.'

Details forgotten, Megan raised a brow. 'Won't he now.' Alexander? The name wasn't familiar. 'Well, I'm afraid he'll just have to. At the moment the schedule for the Burtons' house-sitting requirements take priority over Mr Alexander's demands, whatever they may be. Be an angel, lay on your usual charm; explain as this is a partnership you can deal with his enquiry just as well. If he still won't budge, tell him I'll call him back within the hour.'

'Mind if I press for the second,' Jane responded quickly. 'He sounds really impressive and quite demanding. You're so much better at handling that type of person than I am.'

Megan's mouth curved. Since their first day at primary school when they had formed an immediate bond, Jane had always been the more diffident of the two.

'Jane,' she complained lightly, 'you're perfectly capable of dealing with awk-ward clients and you know it. Not that we've had many, thank goodness. Anyway, how can you tell what he's like from a phone call?'

'You haven't heard him yet!'

Megan wasn't impressed. 'Sounds like one of those muscle-bound body builder types.'

'Yuk!' Jane echoed her distaste. 'No chance. Anyway if I am wrong, you can just concentrate on his masculine tones.'

Megan laughed. 'Now that sounds interesting.'

'Wonders will never cease. I'll put him through.'

'No, Jane,' Megan swiftly insisted. 'I'll ring him back. That's the best I can do right now. By the way, is Stephanie in yet?'

'No. She has a dental appointment, remember? Probably be here around two.'

Megan remembered. 'Of course. In that case could you do your second favour of the day and buy me a sandwich before you break for lunch.

Looks like I'll be taking mine at my desk.'

'Again! OK then. I'd best get back to our caller and get his number,' Jane accepted defeat with a sigh.

As Megan replaced the receiver she was still smiling. Looked like Jane's continuing efforts to sell the opposite sex to her were still going strong. When would she get the message that for the foreseeable future, Time Savers took priority over everything else in her life?

2

Some time later as Megan saved the details of the Burtons' schedule on disc, an abrupt rapping on her office door startled her into looking over from the computer.

She frowned. She wasn't expecting anyone. She got up from her chair and was a moment away from the door when it was thrust open.

'Megan Moore?'

Thrown by the sense of urgency about the tall, broad-shouldered figure filling the doorway, she took a step back. 'Yes,' she acknowledged warily, nonplussed by the frown of impatience above two strong black brows. As his disconcerting grey gaze locked with her china blue eyes, a remembered kick of excitement hit the pit of her stomach.

Something she'd not experienced in years. Something very unsettling.

'Jordan Alexander. Thought I'd save you a phone call.' He glanced around her office. 'I take it you're free now?'

She shook off her confusion and her growing irritation with his manner. 'Er. Yes, Mr Alexander. I am.'

Disguising her thoughts, she stood aside and conjured up a welcoming smile. 'I was just about to call you. Please come in and take a seat.' She gestured towards one of two comfortable chairs placed in front of her desk. 'Can I get you a drink?'

He shot her a glance on his way over to the chairs. 'No thanks,' he said rather brusquely. 'I prefer to get down to business.'

'Of course.' Behind his back, Megan pulled a face. Unprofessional, she knew, but it made her feel she'd scored a point. 'After all, we are here to save people time,' she added as she walked past him around to her own chair.

He remained standing until she sat down. Smile still intact she hooked her pale hair behind her ears and reached for a pen. 'Now,' she asked, 'how can we help you Mr Alexander?'

For a brief moment his grey eyes regarded her dispassionately, while his body language remained still very much that of a man in a hurry. 'I'm here on the recommendation of a friend.'

'Please convey my thanks to your friend.'

He nodded silently. 'I believe you, er . . . get things done for people.'

The slight hesitation was surprising. Whatever his problem, she considered, it must be considerable when he was coming across as someone very much in control.

'We certainly do. The majority of our clients lead busy lives. We're here to ensure what leisure time they do have is not taken up with the more mundane, but necessary part of life . . . from shopping, dental or hair appointments to the more important decisions . . . relocating for example.' She flashed a smile again. 'You could say we're a modern day Jeeves.'

'I see.' So far so good, Jordan considered, as he regarded the woman sitting across from him with hair the colour of just-ripened apricots and eyes reflecting the summer sky.

Despite his grave expression, Megan soldiered on. 'I take it your time is precious too, Mr Alexander?'

Her assumption was confirmed with a grimace. 'It's at a premium at the moment. And running out fast.'

'Oh?' She frowned. That sounded grave. She raised a little more warmth in her expression as she studied his face for any sign of a clue as to why he was feeling so pressurised.

But his grim look didn't alter. 'I've recently acquired a property a few miles outside the village,' he said.

Megan relaxed, the picture immediately becoming clearer. All he was suffering from was a simple case of house-moving panic. She'd seen it before and dealt with it successfully. 'Congratulations. We have some beautiful countryside around here and some very desirable properties.'

'It's been empty for some time,' he continued, ignoring her comment. 'There's some decorating which needs doing before I move in on the twenty-ninth. That's what I want your company to handle.'

'I see.' Megan glanced at her desk calendar. Thirteen days time, she quickly calculated. Pushing it, but not impossible, depending of course on how much the *some* entailed.

'There are twelve rooms in all,' he expanded, 'not including the attics.'

Twelve rooms in thirteen days! She bit back an exclamation and tried not to let her astonishment show.

He had to be kidding, even though he didn't appear to have a sense of humour. But why waste her time like this? 'While we do have professional contacts for this kind of work, Mr Alexander,' she responded coolly, 'I think you're — '

'Not expecting the impossible, Miss Moore,' he sighed, brushing aside her protests with patronising effect and taking the words right out of her mouth.

'All I'm asking for at the moment is some minor restoration and redecoration. Just three rooms to begin with. Oh and the kitchen and first floor bathroom are in need of freshening up. They can be redesigned later. If I'm happy with the standard of work . . . '

Her irritation with him almost reaching boiling point, Megan's brows shot up.

He broke off and gave her a wry look just to let her know her indignation had been noted. 'Perhaps I should re-phrase that. If it works out satisfactory for us both, you'll have the option for the remainder of the work, which I should imagine will take several months to complete. So is your company up to the task, Miss Moore?'

She met his gaze with equal regard. 'Would you be wasting your time if you didn't think we were, Mr Alexander?' she retaliated, hoping desperately that

Jeff Green, the building contractor she used for work of this kind could fit her in.

'Point taken.' His climb down was surprising. The hint of a smile unexpectedly pleasing. 'I suppose I did rather ask for that.'

Megan's irritation eased a little. 'We may be a fledgling company, but I assure you we are not a fly-by-night operation. Not only can we see to your needs for the new property, we would be happy to handle your move too, should you require it.'

He shook his head. 'Not necessary. The furniture is being disposed of. All I'll be bringing to the new property will fill a dozen or so tea chests. Some larger items, antique pieces my grandmother gave me when she downsized are in storage. They will be delivered to the house nearer the time.'

Megan's interest grew. It sounded like Jordan Alexander was at some kind of crossroads in his life.

'Noted.' She quickly jotted this

information down. 'But if you should think of anything else, don't hesitate to get back to us. We're here to help in any way we can.'

She finished her notes then glanced up at him again, disconcerted to see she was being scrutinised once more.

'What I do want you to provide as soon as possible,' he continued, 'are some suggested colour schemes, the right kind of fixtures and fittings to tie in with the age of the house. That kind of thing.'

This came as a something of a surprise. Giving her free range over such personal choices, Megan found was unexpectedly flattering. 'Not a problem,' she smiled.

'It's a country house, Edwardian.'

Her most favourite kind. She experienced a touch of envy. 'Very nice.'

'And you can start?'

'Just let me check for you.' She quickly flicked through her desk diary, her mind racing. Several bookings she'd planned on handling personally could be easily transferred to Jane. Stephanie was always looking for extra hours and was perfectly capable of running things here.

She met Jordan Alexander's grey gaze again. 'I could fit you in Monday morning. The building contractor, I'll check with within the hour. But naturally I'll need to see the property before — '

'Of course.' He dismissed her request with a shrug.

She finished what she was going to say. 'Before I can give you an estimated cost for the initial work.'

'Cost is not important. Time is,' he frowned. 'I have to be in on the twenty-ninth, not a day later you understand.'

She immediately felt on the defensive again. 'You have made that more than perfectly clear, Mr Alexander.'

So he had. He shook off a feeling of tension that had come from nowhere. 'Right. I'll meet you at the house this afternoon . . . ' He glanced at his watch.

'Three o'clock is the best time for me.'

Casually, Megan touched her lips just to make sure she was not by now open-mouthed at his self-centred attitude.

Did he think she sat at her desk all day twiddling her thumbs until someone like him came along? Then again, the speed at which his mind worked was infectious and she found herself eager to view the property.

She made a point of looking back at her diary. 'Yes,' she agreed after a moment. 'Three o'clock is fine.'

'Good. My secretary will fax through a list confirming the initial requirements before then, together with some details of the rooms. This will give you some idea of what's involved before we meet up later.'

Megan nodded her appreciation. 'That will be a help. All I need now is the address and a set of keys if you don't intend to be there while the work if being done.'

'Already in hand. I'll bring them with

me. The house is called Foxcovers and you'll find it on the — '

As his words were lost to a sudden ringing in her ears, Megan experienced the sickly sensation of the colour draining from her cheeks then return with a searing heat.

In a state bordering on shock, she was aware her pen had slipped from her fingers. She flinched as it landed with a clatter on the polished wooden surface of her desk before rolling off on to the carpet.

Jordan Alexander had bought Foxcovers?

Aware her cool exterior was by now thoroughly lost to her flushed cheeks and discomposure, she managed an apologetic smile. 'Sorry about that.' She swallowed against the dryness in her throat.

She had to ask, just in case there was the faintest possibility someone else had come up with the same name. 'That's the large red-brick house just off the top Chester Road.'

He nodded. 'That's the one.'

The raised colour in her cheeks was surprisingly charming, he considered, but then he noticed her eyes were betraying an unexpected tension. His heart sank. Was there something she wasn't telling him? 'Don't say there's a problem already?' he exclaimed.

'A problem? Of course not,' she denied a little too earnestly.

'I get the feeling you know the property.'

Her heart skipped a beat. It was true. No-one could know it better. Although that didn't concern him. She hesitated briefly as she considered how not to tell a direct lie or let it show.

'As you probably realise, this is a small village. It's not difficult to recall certain properties on the outskirts. If I remember correctly,' of course she did, it was imprinted in her heart, 'it's a lovely old house. Distinctive yet not too grand.'

She bit her lip. That was probably the wrong thing to say. Jordan Alexander was coming across as the type of person who probably liked 'grand' things.

Then to her surprise, he nodded in agreement. 'I think so, too. And homely. That's what attracted me in the first place.'

She relaxed a little. But while his opinion raised him a notch in her estimation, she still struggled to come to terms with the news that he was the latest owner of her old family home.

The reclaiming of Foxcovers. The secret ambition she'd held since moving back and starting the business, was snatched from her in an instant. With a heavy heart she cast her longings aside.

'If there's nothing else . . . ' she began to make subtle moves to show their discussion was over. 'I'll see you at Foxcovers at three.'

To her relief he was up from his chair before she had time to push back her own. 'Three it is,' he confirmed.

Beyond the tangle of emotions her mind was still trying to deal with, she remembered her manners and escorted him down the passageway, past Jane's empty office and the small reception area to the front door.

There he paused and offered his hand. She responded automatically. His long lean fingers covered her own and the strength contained in his handshake was somehow all she expected.

She waited until he had stepped out into the high street and closed the door before she walked back into her office. There, a little shakily, she tried to come to terms with what she'd just committed herself to.

So Foxcovers had another owner. Not the first re-sale she'd heard of. The last time it had been run as a private residential home.

And now because of a request for the services of their company, she would be stepping back inside, reacquainting herself, after eighteen years, with memories only allowed to re-surface once in a while.

The only way to see this through, she determined, was to distance herself from her personal history and convince herself Foxcovers was just another project.

Not wanting to dwell on the emotional minefield she would enter later, she cleared her head and reached for the phone. Time to work her charms on Jeff.

A little later, relieved by the builder's positive response and the promise to meet her at the house the following morning to discuss the work, Megan opened a new file on the computer and typed out the notes she'd taken for the Alexander contract.

As she re-checked the details she grimaced. She had made two unforgivable errors — not asking the source of the recommendation or quoting their hourly rate before the enquiry had gone any further.

Placing her elbows on the arms of her swivel chair and she steepled her fingers and stared at the screen. If Jordan Alexander was not agreeable to their terms, at most it would be a wasted journey. That was all.

But on a personal level?

Her eyes became shadowed. Despite the bad memories, the pull of seeing inside her old home was irresistible.

And despite his attitudes, Jordan Alexander was still an intriguing echo in her mind.

The sound of Jane's office door opening cut into her reverie. 'Only me,' Jane called out.

Megan brightened a little, imagining Jane's reaction when she realised she'd just missed their new client.

And when she learned why he was seeking their services? The soft curve of her lips was lost to a frown. Jane was bound to have misgivings that would no doubt equal the ones she was feeling now. But deep down, just to be back at Foxcovers was reason enough to proceed with Jordan Alexander's request.

3

Megan's first sight of Foxcovers' blue-grey roofs, partly screened by full-leafed sycamores swaying lazily in the summer breeze, lifted her heart but at the same time had her pondering Jane's final question as she had left for her appointment.

Had she any idea of what she could be letting herself in for? Pushing her worries aside, she considered instead the faxed lists in her bag. Apart from a first-floor bedroom, listed priority number one, which had 'everything pink' written against it, the planning and choice of colour schemes for the other rooms had been left to her.

So, with the all-pink colour scheme for the bedroom, she mused, Jordan Alexander had to be married. Despite not wearing a ring.

But would she really want to take on

a man like that if he was available, providing she was looking for someone of course . . . which she reminded herself, she wasn't.

The answer was a definite no.

Still, it seemed a little odd that someone like him should go along with such a feminine choice. She shook her head. Just went to show how wrong first impressions could sometimes be.

Despite such girly taste, his wife was either a much stronger character than him. She shivered. Perish the thought. Or he loved her deeply. So it was strange he'd made no mention of her during their meeting.

After all, she was keeping him in the dark about her connection to Foxcovers. And even though this omission niggled like a sore tooth, deep down she was convinced it was the right one.

Just as right as her decision to move back to the area had been. Despite the possibility she might bump into people she once knew . . . with embarrassing consequences.

But this hadn't happened. Those who had recognised her, and how easy that was when she'd inherited her mother's looks and distinctive colouring, had been kind and tactful.

Not that she felt any sense of shame in her past. She felt quite the opposite. But with a contract of this size and importance, there was always the possibility Jordan Alexander might do a little investigation into her personal background as well as the company's.

A small frown marked her brow. For once her change of name could prove a blessing.

Approaching the two stone columns gracing the entrance to the drive, she changed down and turned into it, saddened by the overgrown state of the wide borders either side.

Moments later when the ivy-covered, red-bricked façade rose up in front of her like an old friend, her heart began to thump and her eyes misted with emotion. Blinking furiously, she cast the ache of once belonging here aside.

It came as no surprise to see a top of the range 4 × 4, parked over to the left of the front porch. It went perfectly with her latest client, she reflected.

She pulled up her serviceable Volvo alongside, switched off the engine and checked her watch. Five minutes to three. Perfect.

Aware of the tension building in the pit of her stomach, she picked up her roomy tan leather shoulder bag, which doubled most of the time as a briefcase and climbed out of the car.

While the afternoon sun shone brightly, the stirrings of a cooling breeze ruffled her glistening hair. She shook back its fullness from her face and glanced up, compelled to seek out the far bay window of what had once been her bedroom.

With all kinds of memories vying for selection, a sense of loss returned.

Immediately, despite all her just-made intentions, she felt the pangs of what might have been. At the same time she was aware the front door was opening.

Squaring her shoulders, she turned towards it and found herself experiencing a sudden grip of expectation.

Inside the stone porch, Jordan Lawrence stepped down from the threshold to greet her. 'Miss Moore,' he nodded formally.

'Hello again,' she said, a bright smile firmly in place.

There was no response in his steady regard. What made a man in his mid to late thirties so crusty, she wondered.

'Thank you for coming. I appreciate you must have had to rearrange your diary.'

This acknowledgement came as a pleasant surprise.

'Not a problem,' she assured him.

'Let's get started, shall we?'

With her expression disguising her thudding heart, she took up his invitation. It changed the moment she entered the long sunlit hall and the past came crowding in with numbing force. For a second she faltered. Then blanking her mind to the pain of the past, she continued along the patterned red, black and white tiled floor.

Two steps more and the butterflies in her stomach were sacrificed to a rush of apprehension when the thought suddenly struck her.

For all his bearing and her ready acceptance of what they'd discussed earlier, she didn't know this man from Adam. What had she been thinking of, setting up a meeting with a stranger in such isolation?

She flinched when the solid thud of the front door closing seemed to seal her fate. She turned swiftly and scanned the granite planes of his face. There was something different in his manner since this morning; a preoccupation that was as puzzling as it was disconcerting.

She tensed as he came up alongside her, but tried not to show her anxiety. He gestured with his hand. 'I'd like to begin upstairs.'

As she hesitated, the tones of a mobile phone sounded. Maybe this would turn out to be the means of her escape. She flicked open her bag and dived inside. 'Sorry,' she said.

Jordan didn't look pleased. 'I think you'll find it's mine. Excuse me one moment.' With a grimace of impatience he retrieved the offending object from inside his jacket and switched it on. 'Bear with me,' he instructed the caller brusquely.

Was that frown a permanent fixture, Megan considered as he glanced back at her.

'Business call. Won't keep you a minute.' He nodded towards the staircase. 'Go on up to the first floor while you're waiting. Take a look around and see what you think of the rooms up there.' And with that he disappeared around the nearest door, closing it behind him.

Still ultra-sensitive to the situation, Megan expelled a shaky sigh before leaning back against the wall. If he wasn't the genuine article, she reasoned, he wouldn't have left her alone like this. Concerns fading, she hugged her bag to her, not quite ready to consider the stairs.

As the strength returned to her limbs, she glanced at the closed door of what had once been her father's study, behind which her client was taking his call. Her loss hit home and once more she felt uncertain of how to deal with the weight of association.

She scanned the panelled walls. A handrail at waist level ran along the length of one of them. A reminder of its previous ownership. She took a closer look. This addition appeared to have been carefully done. Its removal, she calculated, should cause little damage.

Then as she raised her eyes to the staircase she gave an expression of disgust. Above the sunlight pouring in through the tall, leaded window on the half-landing, the beautiful plaster mouldings were now a hideous shade of mustard yellow.

'Still here?'

The impatient demand from behind

jolted Megan back to the present. She threw the source of criticism a hasty look and met the usual impersonal gaze.

'Let's get on. I take it you have copies of the lists my secretary faxed through?'

'Yes, of course,' she replied.

With the sure conviction she was being tested and not doing very well, she dived inside her bag again and pulled out a sheaf of papers; annoyed to see a slight tremor of her hand. 'I have them here.'

'Good.'

'Together with . . . ' She reached in again. But when she looked up about to produce her own papers with a flourish, she saw he was half-way across the hall and heading for the stairs. ' . . . some suggested colour schemes,' she muttered with feeling, glaring after him.

'Which we will discuss as we go round.'

She coloured a little when his wry backward glance told her he'd heard every word and picked up on her tone.

34

Increasing her step, she hurried up the stairs after him. Reaching the top she was just in time to see him disappear inside what had once been her parents' bedroom.

Safe from the contemplation of Jordan Alexander's assessing eyes she paused for a moment to take a deep reassuring breath before continuing down the landing.

Fate had brought her back, albeit temporarily, and it was now up to her not to throw away the opportunity of restoring the house to its former glory.

4

As Megan stepped inside the bedroom, Jordan positioned himself in the centre of the square bay window. Behind him a backdrop of grimy, rich blue velvet drapes sagged drunkenly above the window seat. The room's air of neglect, Megan noticed, appeared to enhance his clean-cut image.

'The master bedroom,' he said. As he watched her look around and take in the details, it occurred to him there was an almost haunted look in her eyes. Overwork . . . personal problems? Doubts in her abilities began to niggle but he pressed on. 'As you can see, the décor leaves a lot to be desired.'

Replaced by all that pink? Megan considered. Not a great improvement on the present overblown flowered wallpaper. But then it might just work if his wife chose a combination of subtle shades.

'It is pretty grim, isn't it,' she agreed. 'A neutral colour wash would be much more gentle on the eye.'

'Sounds perfect to me.'

She looked back at him in some surprise. What about the pink?

'I also want the fireplace exposed,' he added. 'Why people buy old houses then attempt to modernise them is beyond me.' He threw a look of disapproval to where the fireplace had been boarded up and papered over.

'And me,' Megan echoed softly, recalling with a stab of pain the cold October day so many years ago when there had been a fire burning in the grate. The day which had proved to be her last at Foxcovers.

'Now let's move on.' He started towards her then added, 'According to what I've learned, this house has something of a chequered history.'

Megan's heart lurched. She'd been right. He was the investigating type. 'Is that so?' She turned her head away, feigning further interest in the room.

'Apparently there have been two attempts to run it as a private residential home,' she heard him say. 'The last attempt didn't even get off the ground.'

Let that be it, she agonised.

'Before that it had remained in the same family it was originally built for.' Her heart sank. She shot him a glance. From his expression she knew what was coming. 'Then about eighteen years ago, they lost the place,' he continued. 'Seems the owner was some kind of forger, would you believe?'

His look of amusement felt like a slap across her face. Hating the mocking curve of his mouth, she found herself retaliating. 'Copyist is more the correct term.' Her bright eyes defied him to argue the point.

He raised a dark brow, but still looked amused. 'Is that right?'

A little more information, she considered heatedly, and he might not find the situation quite so entertaining.

'Gideon Lancaster was not the

common criminal you assume,' she snapped. 'He was a brilliant artist in his own right who happened to find himself in a desperate financial position. At the time his own paintings didn't command the prices they do today so he copied the style of others, claiming they were originals when they were sold.'

Jordan's expression grew thoughtful. 'Interesting.'

Interesting? Megan felt deflated. So much for her defence of her father. 'I'd say tragic,' she argued, too angry to consider she was in danger of throwing the contract away. 'If they had, I very much doubt you would be Foxcovers' new owner and I'd be here advising you on colour schemes.'

As his eyes narrowed and his mouth thinned, she realised she'd gone much too far. Why couldn't she have held her tongue.

In the tension building between them she quickly back-pedalled. 'I'm sorry, Mr Alexander. I shouldn't have said that. You weren't to know what the

Lancasters went through.'

'But you obviously do.' For a moment he studied her strained expression with some interest. 'I take your point. Although in many people's eyes you're still defending a swindler?'

Heat crept over her face. How could she have allowed her feelings to rise above the closely-guarded control she usually kept over them? But then no-one had made her feel this defensive before.

The trauma of what her father had been put through was still making her heart ache but the fight inside was gone. 'Desperate people sometimes act completely out of character,' she said quietly.

She looked away, the blousey crimson roses blurred on the walls. 'He was a good man who found himself in unbearable circumstances,' she added almost to herself. 'It was a tragedy he lost the chance to defend his actions.'

'Why was that?' Jordan regarded her tense profile.

Megan's eyelids fluttered. 'He died of a heart attack before the case came to court.'

'Pity.' So the man hadn't had the chance to argue his case, Jordan reflected. His curiosity was immediately aroused. It might prove an interesting read. And it would be satisfying to see if Megan Moore's loyalties were deserved. If they were, he could tell her. If not he'd probably keep his opinion to himself.

'You're right to take that stance,' he said. 'After all, a person is innocent until proved guilty.'

She swallowed, finding this small show of support gratifying. 'It seems such an injustice.'

'It's life.' He shrugged. 'It happens. I come across desperate people all too often in my line of work.'

Which was, she wondered.

'You appear to know a lot about the case considering you must have been a child at the time?' he said before she had time to ask.

Megan weighed her answer before responding. 'Something like that happening around here was unimaginable. And despite,' she hesitated, this was becoming more difficult than she'd expected, 'or maybe because the Lancaster family was so well liked and respected, it was hard for people to take in. It stays in the mind. No matter . . . ' Once more she felt her composure falter. She looked away again, this time focusing on the trees outside, 'how young or how detached one is from it.'

'Is?' Jordan picked up instantly.

She frowned back at him in some confusion then realised what she'd said. 'Was . . . of course,' she quickly corrected.

Could he sense the lie that was tearing her up inside? Rather than risk further probing, she turned the conversation back on him. 'You're obviously not the superstitious kind, Mr Alexander.'

His frown returned with a vengeance. 'In what sense?'

She shrugged. 'To take on Foxcovers and all its past history.'

He made a small sound of derision. 'Past history for that particular family and its more recent owners. Not mine. I'm a lawyer, Miss Moore. Superstition, luck, whatever you care to call it, plays no part in my life.'

A lawyer. Heaven help anyone facing him in court, Megan contemplated. Then again, to watch him cross-examine would be an experience if the speed and skill at which he'd just considered and questioned what she'd been saying was anything to go by.

'I get my facts right,' he added. His eyes narrowed. 'Do my research thoroughly.'

So his professional skills could not be faulted. But what about his personal life? From out of nowhere came the need to know.

'That way,' he added, 'I avoid any possible complications.' He glanced at his watch then moved towards the door. 'Let's move on to the room that's top of the list, shall we? I have to be on the road in less than an hour.'

Further down the landing, when Jordan stopped outside the very room Megan had once called her own, her mouth went dry.

'Now this one,' he said, 'I'm pretty sure my daughter will like.'

His daughter.

So she'd been right about his married state. With a daughter came a wife. Maybe a son, too? Maybe several?

She had the sudden picture of him in a restored Foxcovers surrounded by a group of beautiful dark-haired children. Hopefully, she reflected, with a lot more laughter in their long-lashed grey eyes than their father had so far shown.

The growing desire to get to know him better, shrivelled and died. 'I've not had time to show it to her yet. What d'you think?'

'It's absolutely perfect,' she answered. 'Well, it will be, once the walls have been stripped and that awful maroon carpet has been taken up. Again, a much softer colour scheme will work wonders.'

This time the corner of his mouth curved as he glanced sideways at her. The transformation took her completely by surprise.

'I agree,' he nodded. 'There's just one small problem. As far as Abbie's ideas go, she'll have any colour as long as it's pink.'

The pink was for in here? Things began to fall into place. 'Ah, that explains it.' Megan smiled, for the first time feeling relaxed. It was Jordan's turn to look bemused. 'The list you faxed,' she prompted. 'The room with everything pink written against it. I thought this was for your bedroom.'

His look of disdain was so comical she couldn't help but chuckle. 'So you and your wife will have a battle on your hands as far as this room goes?'

Her amusement seemed suddenly out of place when she saw him stiffen. Then to her puzzlement, his jaw line hardened and his lips compressed.

A crease appeared between his brows. So much for trying to put things on a personal level, she considered. Pity, as this was the nature of her business and the way she always worked. It had never been a problem before.

'I have no wife, Miss Moore.'

*　*　*

'Good, you're back,' Jane exclaimed when Megan returned soon after five o'clock and popped her head round Jane's door.

Noticing an almost preoccupied manner about her, Jane switched off her computer and took out her bag from the desk drawer. 'I think we should call it a day, Meg. Did everything go all right?'

Megan nodded abstractedly. Jane scanned her expression a little anxiously. 'How about trying Pistachio's?' she suggested. 'It's been open for over a week and we still haven't been inside.

You can tell me how you got on over a cappuccino.'

'What's that?' Megan snapped out of her preoccupation over Jordan Alexander. 'Pistachio's? Yes. Why not?' She gathered her thoughts together. 'Sounds like a great idea.'

The pungent aroma of roasting coffee beans filled the air, when with some curiosity they entered the refurbished premises of what had until recently been a tea room a few doors down from Time Savers.

'Wouldn't have recognised the place,' Jane murmured as they both took in the smooth lines of the pale pine fittings and dark leather chairs.

A young waiter promptly appeared once they'd made themselves comfortable.

While Jane gave their order, Megan gazed unseeingly at the passers-by in the High Street. Jordan Alexander's final bitter words still in the forefront of her mind.

'Meg?' Jane sought her attention. 'I

don't want to keep harping on the same subject, but are you sure you're doing the right thing by taking on the Alexander contract?'

Megan felt a twinge of guilt when she turned and saw that for once Jane's openly friendly face looked troubled.

She met her concern with a wry smile. 'Want the truth?' she asked.

'Of course.' Slighted, Jane's brown eyes widened with surprise. 'Hasn't it always been that way between us?'

'Sorry.' Megan looked suitably chastened. 'Of course it has. I'm not thinking straight.'

'That's exactly what I mean,' Jane exclaimed quietly, conscious of other people sitting nearby. 'I wasn't thrilled about you going out to the house in the first place. Since you got back . . . Oh I don't know,' she sighed with frustration, 'it just feels like it didn't do you any good. Which is completely understandable,' she added as an afterthought.

'I'm fine, Jane. Honestly.' This time

Megan's expression softened. 'Don't look so worried. Although if the tables were turned, I'd probably be saying the same thing to you. It hit me hard being there again, but I'm over that now.'

Jane relaxed. 'Well, that's good to hear.'

'I just have to,' Megan added rationally. 'It could turn out to be our biggest contract yet. Apart from the experience, it would look very impressive on the company's C.V.'

'I suppose you're right,' Jane yielded after giving this some thought. 'But that doesn't solve the problem of how you're going to cope there. I'm worried about you, Meg. You'll be making Foxcovers a home for someone else. Won't that hurt?'

Megan shrugged. 'I gave it a lot of thought on the drive back. Despite everything, there's no getting away from the fact that we've been given something we can't turn down.'

Jane's doubtful look spurred her on.

'Jordan Alexander has given me

almost carte blanche with the restoration and decorations. I've got to do it.' Her eyes became lit with enthusiasm. 'Can't you see. It's a chance in a million.' She hesitated for a moment. 'I know it will never be my home again,' she added quietly, 'but in one way, through the work I'll be supervising and helping out with, I'll still be part of it.'

'Looking at it that way,' Jane sighed, 'I can't argue. But be careful, Meg. You've been through enough already.'

Touched by Jane's concern, Megan reached across and squeezed her hand. 'Everything's under control,' she reassured her, 'so stop worrying,' she added just as two large cups of frothy coffee were set down in front of them.

'So, any plans for tonight?' Jane asked after she'd taken a bite of the crisp biscuit that had come with their drinks.

'Just typing up the notes I made this afternoon. Won't take long — half-an-hour or so.'

'In that case, would you like to come round later? It's such a lovely evening.

I'll get Peter to set up the barbecue. We could open a bottle of wine and toast the success of our latest contract. You spend too much time on your own.'

Megan shrugged. 'You know I like to keep busy. Could we make it another time? All I want to do later is take a long bath and have an early night. D'you mind?'

'Course not.' Jane grinned. 'Thinking about it, that will do you more good.'

'Set me up for tomorrow's meeting with Mr Alexander. He's decided to drive over again,' she explained. 'When I told him I'd be showing Jeff around and discussing the work, he said he'd make it, too.'

'So,' Jane persisted, 'if you can't make it tonight, how about Sunday afternoon. I've got the family coming round. Only the other day Mum was saying it's ages since she's seen you, and if the weather holds, the barbie will be put to good use again.'

'Sunday afternoon it is,' Megan agreed.

5

Curled beneath the soft warmth of her duvet, the sound of a car alarm somewhere in the distance had Megan stirring. Sleepily, she turned her head and focused on the read-out on the alarm clock then came to with a start.

Horrified she had slept through her alarm, she flung back the cover and scrambled out of bed. It was the early hours when she eventually realised what the time was and how tired she'd felt before she made her way to bed.

Annoyed the day had got off to a bad start, she hurried through to the bathroom and switched on the power point for the shower. Altering the temperature setting she braced herself for the shock of cold water and took the quickest shower ever.

With one eye on the clock, she breakfasted quickly on a glass of fresh orange juice while she checked her bag for what she needed. Then flinging it over her shoulder, she raced down the service stairs at the back of the building and hurried over to her allotted parking space.

Inside the car she kept her window down. In this heat, she calculated, her hair should be almost dry by the time she reached Foxcovers.

Moments later, coming to a stop in the high street, she groaned with frustration. Already the weekend traffic was nose to tail.

★ ★ ★

'Not long now,' Jordan encouraged as he and Abbie came to a halt at a deserted junction. He then turned left into another country lane. 'A few more miles and you'll see our new home.'

Alongside him, Abbie pursed her lips and folded her arms. After a moment's silence she shot a glance at her father. 'I just hope I like it.'

53

'You'll love it, angel. Promise. It's the big house I've been looking for us for ages. There are gardens all round and,' he emphasised, 'it has two attics up in the roof. You can use one of them as your own special room to play in if the weather's bad when Jenny comes to stay. How does that sound?'

Abbie wasn't totally won over. She still had a grouse. 'Jenny keeps going on at me about not helping you choose it, you know.' This time her glance was accusing. 'If she knew you've picked which room I'm going to have, well . . . ' She rolled her eyes. 'I'm seven-and-a-half now, Dad. Not a baby.'

Jordan's lips twitched. In a few week's time it was bound to change to seven and three-quarters. 'Of course you're not,' he agreed. 'Anyway, it's not set in stone.'

He could see from her frown she was not sure of his meaning. 'If you don't like the room you can choose another,' he explained. 'But this one is just down the landing from mine. And it's more than twice the size of the one you have now with a great view across the garden and the countryside.'

Abbie gazed up at him. 'With fields and horses in them?'

Jordan nodded, his eyes fixed on the road. 'Some. Yes.'

'S'pose it'll be good then. Especially when I get my own pony like you promised. And a dog. And two kittens.'

'Tell me Miss Alexander,' Jordan made the pretence of being greatly serious, 'when were the kittens added to the list?'

The giggle he expected came, giving him the usual warm feeling. 'Oh, ages ago.'

'One thing at a time, young lady, but yes I did promise,' he quickly pre-empted a flood of protests. 'Once we've sorted out a riding school and lessons and you're sure you like that kind of thing, we'll see about buying a pony.'

Jordan reached over and ruffled Abbie's mass of dark curls. Briefly he met the grey eyes mirroring his own before turning his concentration back to the quiet country lane. It almost choked him how much he loved her.

'The gardens are like Jurassic Park at the moment.' He nudged Abbie's shoulder and grinned. 'You never know, there might be a dinosaur or two lurking about in the undergrowth.'

'Dad!' Abbie's freckled face displayed her disdain. 'Me and Jenny are not into dinosaurs anymore. I told you ages ago. We like whales and dolphins now.'

'Jenny and I,' Jordan corrected gently.

'Sorry.' He looked suitably chastened. 'I forgot.'

'Does the lady who's making it nice for us like the house, too?' Abbie's unexpected question impacted on him with a force that took him by surprise.

Megan's blue eyes, the memory of her smile which he hadn't been able to shake off completely since yesterday, returned again.

★ ★ ★

Arriving at Foxcovers, Megan expelled a sigh of relief to see she was the first there. Then just as she climbed out of her car the familiar sight of Jeff's large blue van with *Green's Building Contractors* picked out in large white lettering on both sides, pulled up alongside.

She waited while he swung out of the cab. His son, David, who worked with him, climbed out of the passenger side.

'Morning Jeff . . . David,' she acknowledged as they joined her.

'Mornin' lass,' Jeff greeted.

It always amused Megan that Jeff continued to regard her, a twenty-six-year-old woman running her own business, as a lass.

'Mr Alexander has decided to drive over, too,' she told the two men. 'So you'll have the chance to meet him and discuss what he wants doing.'

Jeff nodded his grey head. 'Sounds good.'

Megan checked her watch. 'Come

and take a look for yourselves while we're waiting.'

She had just shown Jeff and David into the grimy kitchen when the sound of Jordan calling her name from the hall unexpectedly turned her heart over. She took a breath. 'That's him now,' she said.

As she walked through the alcove at the rear of the staircase, the first thing that struck her was how different Jordan appeared today. Gone was the expensive suit, the pale shirt and dark tie. And the professional bearing.

Instead, blue denim covered the length of his long legs and a navy blue tee-shirt outlined his broad shoulders.

And even though he was turned slightly away from her, saying something to the small child she immediately took to be his daughter, she could sense his relaxed manner.

With a lift of anticipation she closed the distance separating them. 'Good morning, Mr Alexander.'

The moment he turned and his grey

eyes locked with hers, something inside her changed for ever.

'Miss Moore,' he smiled. 'Hope we haven't kept you waiting.'

'Not at all,' she responded, experiencing a strange feeling of breathlessness. 'I was just about to show Jeff and his son, David, what needs to be done in the kitchen. Would you like to come and meet them?'

'Of course,' Jordan agreed. 'But before we do, this is my daughter, Abbie.'

She couldn't be anyone else's, Megan considered as she smiled down at the pin thin figure of Jordan's small daughter dressed in pink jeans, a pink and white striped top, and pink trainers. When his hand rose protectively on to her narrow shoulders, Abbie slipped beneath his arm. She looked up a little uncertainly at him and then glanced again at Megan.

'Aren't you going to say hello?' he encouraged.

'Hello, Miss Moore,' she responded in little more than a whisper.

Megan was touched by her shyness. 'Why not call me Megan,' she offered. 'It sounds more friendly, don't you think?'

Abbie sought assurance from her father. 'I think so, too,' he smiled, his grey eyes twinkling as he looked down at her. 'Don't you?'

Abbie nodded then shot a glance at Megan. 'Megan,' she repeated.

'And may I call you Abbie?'

A smile broke out and Abbie nodded, 'Yes.'

'Right, that's settled,' Jordan said happily.

Megan was delighted that Jordan, Jeff and David hit it off straight away. As their conversation became more involved with building technicalities, Abbie began to hop on one foot to the other as she tried to look out of the nearest window. Megan guessed she was becoming bored.

'How about I ask your dad if we can do some exploring while he's busy, Abbie?' she suggested quietly.

Abbie's eyes lit up. 'Yes, please,' she nodded eagerly.

'Mr Alexander?' Megan grabbed the opportunity when there was a pause in the discussions.

Jordan glanced over.

'Is it all right with you if Abbie and I do some exploring.'

'I want to see my room, Dad.'

'Sounds like a good idea to me.' He glanced at Megan. 'OK if I catch up with you in a few minutes.'

'Of course. When you're ready.'

'See you later, Dad,' Abbie called. 'Ready, Megan?' And with that she headed for the kitchen door.

Once inside the bedroom, Abbie began to explore, while Megan watched with pleasure as the child made her way around. Over at the bay, she called out excitedly, 'Look Megan, it's got a seat all the way round under the window with lids. We haven't any of those in our apartment.'

Megan was touched by her enthusiasm. If anyone was to have her old room, she was glad it was Abbie.

Abbie then knelt down on the plain pine surface. 'It's a bit hard for knees,' she said, 'but OK to sit on if you ever want to try.'

At this apparent invitation, Megan sat down. 'Hmm, I see what you mean. How about some long cushions to make it more comfy.'

Beside her, Abbie traced a pattern in the dust on the windowsill with her finger. 'That would be good.'

'So what colour would you like?'

Abbie didn't hesitate. 'Pink.'

Megan hid a smile. Jordan really did have a battle on his hands. 'Pink is a lovely colour.'

Abbie looked pleased. 'It's my favourite colour in the whole world.'

'I thought it was. But there are other colours just as nice. Sunshine yellow would go well with pink.'

Abbie didn't appear that impressed. 'Not sure.'

'We could always look at some paints and wallpaper for your room, if you like?' Megan pressed on. 'Some of them are very pretty.'

'OK.' Abbie slid off the window seat and skipped into the centre of the empty room.

Abbie looked pleased with herself as she carried on moving around the room. 'What's your favourite colour, Megan?'

'I have two. I like blue and green best.'

Abbie thought for a moment. 'My other favourite's white.' Megan's spirits lifted. Here was another possibility. 'Mummy liked red,' Abbie added unexpectedly, on the move again.

Megan's heart skipped a beat. Could this be her opportunity to discover a little more about the Alexander family history?

6

Megan hesitated, not sure how to go about asking questions of a seven-year-old. Abbie had used the past tense. Jordan had said with feeling he had no wife. Were they divorced? Was his wife dead? 'I see,' she began carefully. 'But she doesn't like red any more?'

When Abbie's expression became sombre and she looked away, Megan cursed her curiosity. Whatever was on the little girl's mind, she was not happy.

'Well . . . ' Abbie said slowly, 'she might still do.' She regarded Megan with a thoughtful expression. 'Can you have favourites in heaven? Mummy died when I was five so there's just Dad and me now. I haven't got a brother or a sister like Jenny. She's got two of each.'

Reading the child's dejection, Megan's heart went out to her. 'Oh Abbie, I'm sorry,' she said. She got up and went over to where Abbie was twisting the doorknob and watching the lock go in and out.

Abbie shrugged then carried on twisting. 'It's all right. I'm used to it.'

With this insight into Jordan's personal life, things were a whole lot clearer. People coped with hurt in many ways. He was obviously still in mourning, cherishing his wife's memory dearly. She must have been someone very special.

'D'you know, Abbie,' she said softly, 'my mummy died when I was just a little bit older than you.'

Abbie regarded her thoughtfully. 'I'm seven-and-a-half so you must have been eight?'

Megan nodded. 'That's exactly right. Well done.'

Abbie looked pleased with her calculations. 'That must have been a very, very long time ago.'

Megan suppressed a smile. She nodded. 'That's right, it was.'

'Dad says Mummy's gone to heaven, and she's safe there. She might know your mummy.'

'You know, she just might,' Megan encouraged, wanting Abbie's natural liveliness to return. 'Now how about exploring some more of your new home? There's lots more to see.'

'Yes. I could see more stairs.' Abbie shivered melodramatically. 'But they looked a bit dark and scary.'

'I expect that's because all the other doors on the next floor are closed and the sunlight can't shine down,' Megan explained. 'So how about we go up together. It won't be at all scary, promise. We can take a look at the other rooms and leave the doors open. Or we can go straight on up to the very top where the attics are. I'm sure you'll like them. One of the attics is where — '

Her heart tightened. She was just about to tell the child all about her father's studio. 'Is very sunny and light,' she swiftly amended, 'because of all the big windows.'

And oh how much she wanted to see it again.

'The attics, please.' Abbie slipped her hand into Megan's, leaving her touched by her need for reassurance. 'I think I'd like that first. Jenny doesn't have attics.'

Megan couldn't contain her curiosity any longer. 'Who's Jenny?' she asked with a smile.

'My best friend in the whole world. And I'm older by one day.'

The moment she opened the door and walked on to the paint-splattered floorboards, Megan was aware of the unmistakable scent of oil paint still lingering in the long sunlit room and was immediately swept back in time.

Abbie wriggled her nose. 'There's a funny smell in here,' Megan heard her say. Briefly, she closed her eyes against the memories. This wasn't such a good idea after all. She should have left Jordan and Abbie to discover the attics for themselves.

'D'you know what it is, Megan?'

Her eyes snapped open. 'It's oil

paint, Abbie. The man who lived here a long time ago painted beautiful pictures.'

Abbie frowned. 'Why aren't there any in the house then?'

Megan hesitated. What should she say? She was loathe to lie to a child. 'They were taken away and sold,' came a voice from behind.

Megan's stomach flipped. Jordan! With the past back in the recesses of her mind, she turned warily to see him coming into the room.

'Dad!' Megan was abandoned. With a whoop of joy Abbie darted off to greet her father. She grasped his hand and pulled him farther inside.

'I wondered where you two ladies were hiding. Are you having a good time, sweetheart?'

Abbie nodded. 'It's great, Dad. Megan said I'd like this room with all the big windows.'

No. Megan's heart sank. She'd been far too careless again.

'And I do. Even though it's got a

funny smell. Megan said it's oil paint.'

Megan tensed as Jordan shot her a look, the smile he was giving his daughter replaced by a small frown. How could she have been so thoughtless to have let her guard slip again, even to a seven-year-old?

She could tell his analytical mind was already asking questions. She got in first. 'An artist's studio needs a northern light . . . lots of it if possible. The attics are perfect.'

Jordan's response seemed a long time coming. Then he said, 'You'd put Sherlock Holmes to shame with your deductions. Is that the secret of your success?' One side of his mouth curved, but his raised brow hinted he wasn't really joking.

Still, it looked like she'd got away with it again. She couldn't believe her luck.

Abbie lost interest in their conversation and slipped her father's hold. She darted over to the long window space to look out at the view.

Jordan strolled over to where Megan was standing. He regarded her thoughtfully. 'You're a woman of many talents. You seem to know a lot about the subject.'

'I took art history at college,' she explained.

'Megan,' Abbie interrupted. She began to gesture excitedly. 'Come and look. There are horses in the fields over there.'

'In a minute,' Jordan called over his shoulder. Even though his tone was relaxed, Megan felt she was under the spotlight again. 'So d'you dabble in your spare time?'

'What? Me?' This time her answer would come straight from the heart. 'I'm not blessed with those skills, Mr Alexander. Hence the more academic route. But I've always had an interest in art.'

'It shows.' She wasn't sure how to take this. Then he smiled. 'Jordan, please. If you're on first name terms with my daughter, surely we can share that, too?'

She matched his expression. 'I don't see why not.'

'And that's how you've come to retain such an interest in the infamous Gideon Lancaster?'

Her heart lurched against her ribs. She might have known he wouldn't be so easily accepting. Her gaze went everywhere in an attempt to slip his. 'I . . . I expect so,' she hedged.

'I see. And — '

'Megan! Dad! C'mon.' Abbie gestured frantically. 'They're starting to move away.'

Megan thanked heaven and Abbie's impatience for the chance to side-step Jordan's probing, but she had the ominous feeling she was still not off the hook.

The half-considered idea he'd had of researching the Lancaster case was growing. Jordan made a mental note to give Diane a call when he had a spare minute. See what she could turn up.

Megan chose to stand to the right of Abbie. Jordan took the left. Under the pretence of admiring the view, from the corner of his eyes and above her line of vision, he watched every feminine gesture she made as she spoke to his daughter.

He noticed how her face lit up as she followed the direction in which Abbie was pointing. The way her blue eyes sparkled.

'Dad!' He felt a tug on his arm and pulled his thoughts in order.

'Yes, Abbie?'

'Can Megan come round the rest of the house with us?'

'Megan might have other things to do, Abbie. She's a very busy lady.'

Abbie's look of disappointment made him feel a real killjoy. He caught Megan's eyes. 'Do you have the time?'

'I have the rest of the day, if that's long enough for you.'

Abbie beamed. 'Good. You're coming too, Dad, aren't you?'

Jordan hesitated. 'I've just remembered something else I need to talk to Mr Green about. Don't worry. It shouldn't take long,' he hastened when he saw Abbie's face fall. 'I'll catch up with you both in a little while . . . promise.'

Abbie sighed. 'But your little whiles aren't little. They're long.'

The sight of Jordan's pained expression had Megan coming to his rescue. 'Abbie, we could explore the garden, while we're waiting for your dad. Who knows what we might find out there?'

Abbie pursed her lips, battling against the disappointment of not having her dad with her the whole time and feeling excited about her new friend. 'Dad said it's like Jurassic Park,' she told Megan.

Megan offered her hand to Abbie. 'Let's go and see what we can find.'

* * *

'You could just about squeeze through, I suppose,' Megan agreed a little doubtfully.

She weighed up the narrow space

between the weathered wooden door set in the high sandstone wall just visible behind a rampant bramble thicket which Abbie was all for going behind.

'But there's no way I could. And I'd rather not take the risk of you becoming tangled up in those thorns. Your dad would never forgive me.'

'Oh no!' Abbie exclaimed with feeling. 'I wanted to see what's behind that door.'

Megan knew exactly, but wasn't saying. It opened on to the walled garden and the summer house. Both had played such a precious part of her own childhood and their discovery a surprise she'd been saving for Abbie at the end of the child's explorations.

She'd been careful to make no mention of it, planning on it appearing as Abbie's find. But the thicket had put an end to her idea.

'But I'd be extra careful so he wouldn't have to forgive you.' Abbie tried again. 'Please, Megan. I want to see.'

Megan applied a little diplomacy. 'Why don't we go find your dad and ask him what he thinks about it.'

'You bet,' Abbie exclaimed, darting on to the path again. She paused and gave Megan a thoughtful look. 'But I'll go first 'cos there's something else I want to ask him.' And with that she set off in a flash. 'See you in a minute,' she called over her shoulder, swiftly skirting an overgrown rhododendron weighed down with a mass of white blooms.

Watching the slight figure running towards the house, Megan smiled, wondering what the something else could be? With that little girl's zest for life, she decided, it could be anything.

At one with nature and feeling the pleasurable heat of the summer sun on her back, Megan sensed a burgeoning restlessness.

Less than twenty-four hours ago her life-plan was running smoothly, and now she wasn't sure where she was heading.

What had changed? She frowned.

Everything and probably nothing.

'Megan, please say you'll come.' Abbie's breathless request as she came racing back around the shrubs diverted Megan's thoughts.

Jordan was hot on the heels of his eager daughter.

'Come where?' Megan asked.

'To have lunch with us of course.'

So that was it. Surely Jordan wouldn't want her taking up any more of his time. She'd make the decision for him. 'I really don't think I can, Abbie.' Abbie's face dropped. 'Your dad might have made plans for just the two of you.'

'But he hasn't,' Abbie enthused. 'You said if it was OK with Megan, it was fine by you, didn't you, Dad?'

Jordan nodded. 'Yes I did, but I also said,' he gave her a gentle reminder, 'Megan might already have made arrangements for lunch.'

Is he offering me a get-out, Megan wondered. Then in the depths of his eyes she had her answer.

'Not today,' she said, a little huskily.

'So you will come?' Abbie took her hand. It was the distraction she needed. The child's face was a picture of longing.

'Of course. I'd love to.'

'Good,' Jordan said. 'That's settled then.'

As she welcomed Jordan's enthusiasm, a small voice niggled. She had to distance herself from this man and his delightful daughter before it all ended in tears.

Abbie offered her other hand to her father. 'C'mon,' she instructed. 'Let's go now, Dad. My tummy's rumbling.'

'Jeff and David have just left,' Jordan addressed Megan, 'so there's nothing to keep us here. Does now suit you?'

'Now's fine,' she said, aware of Abbie's eagerness to be off.

Once Jordan made sure Abbie had secured her seat belt, he ushered Megan into the front passenger seat of the 4 × 4.

There she watched as with one fluid

movement he swung himself up behind the wheel. He turned to her before firing the engine. This time his smile was a little warmer. 'Right Megan, is there anywhere in particular you can recommend to two newcomers.'

'Town's filled with summer visitors right now,' she said smiling back. 'Parking could be tight. Finding somewhere to eat could be even more of a problem. Maybe a country pub? There's one not far from here.'

7

Just outside the next village and with the help of Megan's directions, Jordan soon found the Black Horse complete with thatched roof and a beer garden at the back where meals were being served.

Abbie chose one of the picnic tables set out along the paved terraced. With one eye on the children in the play area, she insisted on sitting next to Megan. Jordan sat across from them.

Megan took the menu. 'Have you seen something you like?'

Abbie shuffled a little closer. She shielded her mouth with her hand and whispered, 'Burger and chips. But Dad'll prob'ly say no.'

Megan glanced across at him. His expression said he'd go along with it. 'But he might say yes,' she whispered back, knowing he could hear every word. 'Because today is special, isn't it? You've seen your new home for the first time.'

Two thoughtful grey eyes regarded her for a minute. 'Yes, I have,' Abbie agreed. She turned her attention back to her father. 'Dad, please can I have burger and chips with red sauce?'

'Can't argue with that now, can I.'

'Yes!' whooped Abbie, exchanging victory glances with Megan and going on to tell her of Jordan's 'great' cooking skills.

Jordan was touched by his daughter's embellishment. It was great all right when it came to frying an omelette or using the microwave, and eating out with Abbie had become a regular routine. She seemed to enjoy it, yet he was left with the feeling she was missing out on home-cooked meals.

'Dad!' Jordan blinked, distracted by the sound of Abbie's voice. 'The lady's here,' she hissed.

Glancing up to his right, Jordan saw the young waitress poised at his shoulder, pad and pencil at the ready. He grimaced. 'Sorry.'

His apology was accepted with a smile and a slightly breathless, 'Would you like to order, sir?'

'Yes. I think we're all ready now.'

Their drinks arrived first. Mineral water for the adults, a 'just for once' cola for Abbie who was by now in seventh heaven.

'Dad's taking the whole of the school holidays off this time,' she told Megan, between long pulls at the plastic straw. 'Aren't you, Dad?'

Jordan nodded. 'That's right. A week Wednesday we're going to have six weeks of quality time. Fixing the house and taking time out.'

'Can Megan come, too?' Abbie interjected swiftly.

Jordan shot Megan a look that said this child of mine is getting out of hand. 'Now slow down, young lady,' he waved a finger at his daughter's pleading expression. 'Megan is going to be very busy working on the house for us and

81

she also has to see to the needs of all the other people she works for. We can't have her to ourselves all the time.'

'Your dad's right, Abbie,' Megan echoed, giving Jordan her support. 'I can't leave my business for too long.'

'But can't you have a holiday and make someone else do all the work?'

'Let's leave it for now, Abbie,' Jordan warned as the waitress arrived with their meals.

While they ate, Abbie kept her head down and had no more to say.

'So Abbie, what d'you like best in school?' Megan took a shot at restoring the relaxed exchanges they'd had before.

'I like music and movement and games and swimming and nature studies . . . and reading,' Abbie rattled off. 'But,' she grimaced, 'I hate arithmetic and having to write neatly. Although Miss Jacobs says my writing's getting much better. Didn't she, Dad?'

Jordan nodded. 'Yes she did. But you must keep practising.'

'I'll do some more when we get home.' Abbie took another bite of her burger.

Schoolwork at the weekend? Megan was surprised. Abbie seemed rather young for that. 'You're a hard worker, Abbie,' she said.

Abbie grimaced. 'Well, I didn't quite finish last night and it's Maxine's party tomorrow. And Dad said if I didn't do it all I'd be in trouble.'

'Oh.' Megan raised an eyebrow at Jordan.

'Not with me,' he protested.

'With Miss Jacobs,' Abbie finished for him after the last chip disappeared. She put down her fork and swiped a paper serviette across her mouth. 'Dad, may I be excused? I want to play now.'

'You may. But don't go too crazy,' he warned.

'I will.' Abbie ran off towards the climbing frame and was soon chatting to another little girl who was about to start up.

With Abbie gone, Megan was aware

of the silence growing between herself and Jordan as they watched Abbie's interaction with the other child. 'You must be very proud of her,' she said.

He nodded. 'I am. She means everything to me.'

Megan smiled. 'I had noticed. It can't be easy coping on your own. Abbie told me about your wife and I'm very sorry for your loss.'

As soon as the words left her lips and she saw Jordan's eyes narrow, she knew she'd said the wrong thing.

The relaxed expression she had been enjoying was lost to the grim setting of his jaw. 'There's no need to be,' he dismissed abruptly.

Jordan shot her another glance, his expression guarded, then got to his feet. 'Looks like we're all finished here. Would you mind keeping an eye on Abbie while I go and settle the bill, then I'll drive you back to your car.'

Megan regarded him steadily. His hard tone and stiff attitude both puzzled and angered her.

While he waited for his credit card to be processed, Jordan thrust his hand in his pocket as the urge to crash his fist against the counter threatened to take over. For the second time in two days he cursed his instinctive reaction to what had been a completely innocent remark on Megan's part.

Why? Why act like that, he asked himself, his mouth set. He couldn't fathom it. He'd had time enough to get over Claire.

It had to be the anniversary coming up the following week that was playing havoc with his subconscious, he decided. Megan's innocent reminder of that night and everything that went with it, was bringing the bitterness he'd felt at the time back to the surface.

The irony it should be aimed at the one person who had impacted on his life so unexpectedly, didn't go unnoticed. Somehow he was going to have to make it up to her and when the time was right, explain the circumstance.

For a moment he baulked at the

thought. By doing so, she would be the only other living person who knew the true facts. Apart from Abbie, of course. Again the familiar worry niggled as he wondered what memories she might have of that night.

Still fuming over the way Jordan had spoken to her, Megan walked over to Abbie, anticipating her disappointment and hating to be the one who had indirectly caused it.

For the child's sake she was sorry the day had ended so abruptly and on such a sour note. The journey back to Foxcovers would be nothing like their drive out.

Still puzzling over Jordan's anger, she reached the metal climbing frame. Abbie was perched on the top with her new friend.

'Hi, Megan,' Abbie called down excitedly. 'This is great. We're having lots of fun.'

Which is about to end. Megan sighed softly. 'Abbie,' she called. 'I'm sorry, but it's time to go. Your dad wants to get back to the house.'

Abbie's shoulders slumped with disappointment. 'But I've only been here a minute,' she complained. She stayed put regarding Megan with a frown. 'You said you had the rest of the day.'

Which was true, Megan recalled, feeling a sudden rush of guilt. Never make a promise to a child you can't keep.

'Abbie!'

Megan stiffened, distracted by the curt tone of Jordan's voice. Still angry and confused by his attitude she could hardly bring herself to acknowledge him.

'It is very wrong to cheek Megan like that,' he thundered. 'Apologise please.'

Megan gave him cold regard. 'It isn't necessary,' she muttered. 'Abbie does have a point.'

'Whether she has or not,' Jordan insisted, keeping his voice low, 'I'll not have her speaking to you like that.'

By now Abbie looked close to tears. She looked from her father to Megan.

'Sorry, Megan,' she muttered.

When she saw the child's bottom lip tremble, Megan wanted to take her in her arms. But all she knew she could do was give her a reassuring smile. 'And I'm sorry things have changed and we have to leave so soon,' she comforted. 'Maybe we could do this again another day.'

If she was taking liberties, she didn't care. She hoped this went some way to ease Abbie's misery and make her father feel the spoil-sport he was.

'Can we all come again next week, Dad?' Abbie asked cautiously. Megan was relieved to see the beginnings of a smile on the child's face. Sulking didn't appear part of this little one's make up. All credit due to her father, she accepted reluctantly.

'We'll see,' Jordan said gruffly. 'As much as we'd like it, Megan might not be free.'

'I'll have to check my diary, Abbie,' she said, concentrating on the child.

'Wicked.' Abbie's natural enthusiasm

was back. 'We could always come out to our new house after school 'til we break up on Wednesday,' Abbie suggested brightly.

Megan wondered how Jordan was going to handle this one.

'I suppose we could,' he said thoughtfully. 'What d'you think, Megan?' He gave her a wary glance. Despite her sensitivity she couldn't help but mellow a little. 'After all you do have to eat.' He arched a dark brow and waited.

She sensed this was his way of saying sorry, let's try again.

She answered him through his daughter. 'I'm sure I can manage that, Abbie, if it's what you'd like.'

'You bet,' Abbie enthused. She looked up at her father. 'We can come again, can't we Dad?'

'Of course.'

Megan watched Jordan ruffle Abbie's hair and the look in his eyes as he regarded his daughter touched something deep inside her.

Just when she thought she'd broken through that cold surface and seen the real man beneath, the shutters came down again leaving her with the feeling of being very much on the outside.

8

Hot and bothered and needing some fresh air inside the room, Megan hooked a shaft of hair behind her ears in an attempt to cool her heated face and made a mental note to wear it up in a pony tail in future when the weather was so hot.

She reached up and tried again, but the painted-over window catch in Abbie's room refused to budge. She glared at the cause of her frustration. Force it any further and there was every likelihood it would come off in her hand.

She expelled a growl of annoyance. What she needed was some lateral thinking or alternatively, someone with a logical brain.

As if in answer to her thoughts, a flash of movement outside on the drive caught her eye. She watched with some disbelief as Jordan's 4×4 came out of nowhere, take the curve smoothly and come to a halt in front of the porch next to where her Volvo was parked.

Megan froze. Then her heart kicked in again. What was he doing here? Yesterday he'd told her he had packing to do?

She drew back again when she heard the vehicle door slamming, wondering momentarily if he was alone.

'Megan?' Moments later, the familiar deep tones were carried up from the hallway and washed over her as they echoed around the empty space.

Despite last night's firm intentions to consider Jordan purely as a client and nothing more, she tried to quench the affect his arrival was having on her.

Closing her eyes briefly, she called out, 'Abbie's room.'

Hearing the thud of footsteps on the uncarpeted stairs she immediately went into action. Window catches forgotten, she flicked her hair from behind her ears before finger-combing it as best she could.

Try as she might, the dust marks on the front of her white T-shirt refused to budge, even after a hasty brushing with the flat of her hand.

She stopped. What was she doing?

She took herself in hand and hooked her hair back again growing more conscious of the stifling heat in the room. Fresh air was what was needed, not concern about the picture she presented to him.

As she turned back to the window and tried another catch, she realised from the clearer tones of Jordan's voice, whoever was with him was not a child. Her brow furrowed. Who could it be?

'Don't tell me you're working today, Megan?'

Of course her heart hadn't listened to her head. The jovial enquiry sent it lurching against her ribs. She turned to acknowledge him and it thudded again. His grey sweatshirt was the perfect match for his eyes.

'Still it couldn't have worked out better,' he added turning slightly to usher in a very attractive woman.

She was dressed casually in beige cotton trousers and matching flat shoes. A shapely mint green top highlighted her long dark hair which rested softly on her shoulders.

And while a tiny frown of curiosity furrowed Megan's brow as to who his companion might be, at the same time she was conscious of her own grubby appearance.

The woman's smile was naturally warm and friendly.

'Megan, I'd like you to meet Diane Chambers,' Jordan began the introductions. 'Diane brings a lot of order into my life. I'd be lost without her. Even though,' he added, 'she's been nagging me for weeks to let her see the house.'

The meaningful look which then passed between the couple immediately made the sun go out on Megan's day. 'Diane, Megan Moore.'

'It's good to meet you at last,' Diane

94

greeted, walking over and offering her hand.

Megan swiftly wiped hers on the side of her T-shirt before responding. 'Sorry,' she grimaced. 'I seem to be attracting the dust today.'

'Don't worry about it,' Diane smiled. 'I'll probably pick up some too on our way around. It's a pleasure to meet you. Jordan's been singing your praises almost as much as Oliver.'

He had? That came as some surprise. And Oliver . . . who . . . ? Then she remembered. 'Oh, Oliver Collins,' she exclaimed. She shot a glance at Jordan. 'He was the person who recommended us to you.' It all clicked into place.

Jordan nodded. 'The same. Apparently he found you on the Internet before moving up North.'

After the general chatting, Megan sensed Jordan's manner change as he focused on her again. 'So Megan, if you're not working, what brought you out today?'

'Just taking the opportunity for a

final look around while there were no distractions,' she said, covering the real reason.

'I'd say that was work,' Jordan joked.

'I suppose you could,' Megan smiled, leaving it at that.

'And now we've come along and ruined it for you.'

'Of course you haven't,' she said briskly. 'You've every right to be here.'

He nodded. 'I must admit the house is taking a hold on me. I'm lucky to have it.'

Her eyelids flickered. 'I'd feel exactly the same.' Her smile was wistful but her eyes were steady. 'You're definitely the right person for Foxcovers. And I know you're going to treat it well.'

'No question. It's the perfect house to raise a family.'

And would Diane have a part in this, she wondered. The feeling of envy this question brought was unsettling. 'Then I'm pleased you've got what you want.'

It was time to change the subject. She lightened her tone. 'By the way, did you manage to finish your packing?'

Jordan looked a little sheepish. 'I'll try to get round to it later, after I've dropped Diane home. But if I still can't work up the enthusiasm for sorting through my life before next weekend, I can always hand it over to you, can't I?'

Megan stiffened. Hand his life over to her? She cleared her head. With a woman like Diane who obviously meant a great deal to him, he meant his packing of course.

She cleared her throat. 'No problem. We can easily arrange that for you.'

'I'll try not to be too demanding of your time.'

'And with that in mind,' Diane prompted. 'I think we should let Megan get on with whatever it is she wants to do while you show me around.'

'All done,' Megan said. 'Actually, I was just about to leave.'

'Before you go,' Diane hastened, 'is there a bathroom here in working order?'

'Yes, of course,' Megan answered.

97

'Along the landing. Last door on the right.'

Diane smiled at them both. 'Won't be a minute.'

'Thanks for coming out today, Megan but we mustn't keep you any longer,' Jordan said when they were alone.

Was that a hint of regret in his voice, she pondered, then swiftly told herself she was being foolish. 'That's OK.' She checked her watch. 'Time I wasn't here.'

'You have a date?'

She hesitated. Why tell him there was no man in her life. And the way things were, there wasn't likely to be for a long time to come. 'Something like that,' she said lightly.

She turned to the window seat to pick up her bag and the large notepad she'd brought to jot down any new ideas she might have had as she'd explored the house, missing the frown her answer caused.

As she shortened the gap between

them she noticed Jordan's expression had changed. 'Is something wrong?' she asked.

'There's something in your hair . . . something black.'

She froze. 'Not a spider,' she breathed.

'Don't think so. Here let me.' He reached up, his light touch felt almost like a caress. Megan closed her eyes briefly as she struggled to overcome the effect this had on her senses.

'It's paint,' he announced with some amusement. 'Flakes of black paint. But how they managed to get there . . . ?'

Megan's face grew warm as she recalled her attempts to tidy her appearance. 'I was trying the window catches earlier,' she explained. 'Must have come off them.'

She looked up. His amusement had changed to studied concentration. 'There, that's the last.' He took her hand in his and turned it over. Then he dropped a scattering of black flakes on to her palm.

She was just about to slide her hand free to dispose of them when he raised it to his lips.

Robbed of speech, Megan watched, then he blew the flakes away. He let her go.

Somehow she managed a shaky, 'Thanks. I'll probably see you sometime in the week.'

'No probably about it. Bye, Megan.'

His promise stayed in her mind as she left the house and slid into her car. Then telling herself with Diane in his life, any comments or promises he made to her could only be in a business sense, she sighed deeply and drove off.

9

'Morning, Megan.' It was a little after eight-thirty on Monday morning when Jane walked into Megan's office. 'Mum and Dad were delighted to see you yesterday.'

'Hi Jane,' Megan greeted, distracted momentarily from the work schedules in front of her. 'Me, too. I really enjoyed catching up with them. Enjoyed the whole afternoon,' she added.

'Looks like it did you good.' Jane grinned coming over to Megan's desk, choosing one of the easy chairs to sink into. She peered at Megan's desk awash with paperwork. 'Remember all work and no play — '

'I know,' Megan sighed. 'After the good time yesterday, I fully intend to take things easier at the weekends once the Foxcovers project is finished.'

'Good,' Jane approved. 'I take it those

are the work schedules.'

'Yes. Jeff and I agreed them on the phone Saturday evening.' Megan then gave Jane a sheepish look. 'I finished them off last night after I got back from yours.'

Jane pursed her lips but didn't pass any comment. 'So everything went smoothly on Saturday? I didn't get a chance to ask you yesterday. Is our latest client happy with everything?'

'Appears to be.' Megan pushed the memory of Jordan's rapid change of mood at the Black Horse. 'He got on well with Jeff. His daughter, Abbie, came along, too. She's a joy. Seems very happy with her new home.'

And what about Diane, a small voice niggled. Where does she come in Jordan's life?

She checked her watch. 'And now I've some phone calls to make before I drive out there. I'll try and get back to the office before you shut up shop each day, but right now I just don't know what will happen.'

'No problem,' Jane assured her. 'I'll ring your mobile if anything urgent crops up. Stephanie will be here of course for back-up. The way things are going we might need her on a full-time basis.'

Megan nodded. 'That's something else we'll have to discuss soon. In the meantime . . . ' She reached for the phone. 'I'd better get started on these calls.'

The enquiries she made proved promising. A panelling expert in Ross-on-Wye was more than willing to drive out that morning to give his advice on the removal of the handrails in the hall.

The wallpaper and fabric specialists, based in Stockport, had a wide range of samples for Jordan and Abbie to peruse at the house. All she needed to do was to call to the shop and collect them.

The buzz of the intercom interrupted her thoughts. 'Yes Jane?'

'I know you're pressed for time and I

won't keep you a minute, but I've just had the secretary of Millers' M.D. on the line. It's another biggie.'

'Millers . . . the textile company?'

'That's the one.'

What could the main local employer possibly want with their small company? Her curiosity was sparked. 'What is it they're after?'

'Apparently,' Jane began to explain, 'the firm's fiftieth anniversary is coming up next month. The owners are presenting every employee with a souvenir crystal goblet. They want to know if we do a gift-wrapping service. I explained our raison d'être and confirmed we could meet their deadline.'

'Sounds a good one,' Megan responded happily. 'As a matter of curiosity, how many employees are we talking about?'

'Three hundred and twenty-five to be exact.'

'That many.' Megan's eyes widened. 'We'll have to call in some of our temps. Let me know later how you get on. I've one more call to make and then I'll have to get round to Foxcovers. Jeff's expecting me.'

Was it her imagination, she wondered as she pulled up outside the house, or was there a different air about her old home already?

Inside the kitchen, work was under way. On top of a run of planks which spanned two step-ladders, two of Jeff's men were washing down the ceiling and walls with sugar soap before they could begin to undercoat them.

'Boss's making a start in the bathroom,' one of them said after Megan had wished them both a cheery good morning.

Pleased the work had begun, she hurried upstairs. Sounds coming from Abbie's room told her it was being tackled too.

She went straight to the bathroom to find Jeff. In her mind's eye she could already see it fitted out with copies of white Edwardian ceramic ware, their exposed pipework and freestanding bath faithful to the originals.

'Morning, Jeff.'

'Mornin' lass,' Jeff responded as she popped her head around the door. He was dressed in white overalls; an old flat cap protected his head. 'Reckon I'll have everything undercoated up here by this afternoon. We'll tackle the master bedroom first thing tomorrow.'

'That'll be great. Thanks, Jeff. I'd better take the drapes down now and get them out of the way for you. After I've dropped them off at the dry cleaners, I'll be around for the rest of the day if you should need me.' She produced her most beguiling smile. 'By the way, d'you have a set of steps I could borrow?'

Warned the set brought out from the van were an old pair they didn't often use, Megan rectified the wobble on one of the worn legs by wedging a wad of folded paper beneath it. Balanced on top in Jordan's room, it didn't take long to unclip the few remaining hooks holding the drapes.

She already knew the blue velvet was

in surprisingly good condition, but pulled a face at the thick layer of dust and the dead spiders caught in the folds.

She was loading the drapes into the back of her car when the sound of a vehicle arriving sent a flutter of butterflies in her stomach.

But it turned out to be a van from the electricity suppliers. She swallowed her disappointment.

When she arrived back from town, Megan had another battle with disappointment. No sign of Jordan's 4×4, just another transit van parked outside the house.

She pulled up alongside and switched off the ignition. For a brief moment she considered what to do next. Jeff would eventually paint the stuccoed ceiling in the drawing-room. The panelled walls and leaded casement windows only needed a thorough clean. The three cleaning ladies she called on when needed would see to that.

The cushioned window seat would

need re-upholstering to match the drapes, once Jordan had approved a colour and design, of course, which she was sure wouldn't be a problem.

And he'd better be quick about choosing some furniture or he and Abbie would be eating off packing cases and sleeping on the floor.

Lost in thought, her heart lurched as someone rapped on her car window. Startled, she glanced up to meet Jordan's wonderful smile through the glass.

'Coming in?' he gestured.

Where on earth had he appeared from, she wondered as her heart did its usual somersault. She nodded and reached for the door, but he already had it half open.

'Hello,' she greeted starting to get out. He cupped her elbow and helped her. 'I've just dropped your bedroom curtains off at the dry cleaners. Once Jeff has given the room a neutral wash of paint, and they're re-hung, it will be transformed.'

He closed the car door while Megan dropped the keys into her bag and then swung it on her shoulder. 'I'm glad you could make it this morning,' she said. 'There's something we need to sort out pretty quickly.'

He grimaced. 'Good or bad. You've got me worried.'

'Well, you shouldn't be,' she protested good-humouredly. 'What are you doing about furniture? You mentioned you were not bringing any from the apartment.'

'That's right. It's all going to charity.' He nodded towards the transit. 'Hired that to bring out a few bits and pieces plus a camping table and some fold-up chairs which I've already set up inside.'

So that was how he'd got here.

'I noticed yesterday you'd been using the window seat to work on,' he continued. 'Couldn't have been comfortable. You'll be able to use the table for the time being.'

'Thanks for that,' she acknowledged. 'It'll come in handy for my laptop.'

'Re-discovered a stack of camping equipment that's been stored in the spare room for years,' he added. He shrugged. 'Claire wasn't the outdoor type.'

Megan sensed immediately by the slight change in his manner that Claire was his late wife.

Then the tension seemed to leave him and the warmth returned to his eyes. 'Anyway, Jeff tells me the electricity's connected, so that can be crossed off the list. Just so happens I brought a spare electric kettle and a small fridge that's never been used.' He looked quite pleased with himself. 'And I remembered to bring tea, coffee, etc. So let's take a quick break.'

The small melamine-topped camping table couldn't accommodate Jordan's long legs, so he sat side on resting his forearm on it.

Across from him, Megan cradled the mug of coffee which he had insisted on making. 'This chair is really comfortable,' she remarked with some surprise.

'Yes, I'd forgotten how much,' Jordan agreed. 'Like I said, they've hardly been used.'

Megan saw an opportunity she just had to take. 'Claire was your wife,' she asked a little gingerly, still conscious she could be treading on very thin ice.

A frown marked his brow, but it was nothing like the thunderous one she'd experienced on Saturday. He nodded. 'She was. We married not long after I'd gained my law degree. I met her during a course placement with her father's firm. A permanent post was held over until I graduated. But it didn't work out.'

He grimaced. 'Bit of a sore point at the time as I was told in no uncertain terms that I was being nurtured for great things. But corporate law is not my style. I'm far happier with the domestic and criminal aspect.'

Megan shifted position a little, unsettled now as to where their conversation might lead.

'And without sounding immodest,'

his eyes sparkled, 'I do have a fair reputation in court.' He paused for a moment then said, 'Once Abbie and I are settled here and I'm back at work, what d'you say to spending a day watching how the legal system operates?'

Megan looked down into her mug. 'I'm not sure I'd feel comfortable watching you persuade a jury to send someone to prison,' she said quietly.

'Send!' His recoil surprised her into looking up at him again. A deep frown marked his brow. 'What makes you think I work for the Crown Prosecution Service?'

She took in his sober expression with some confusion. What indeed? 'I suppose . . . ' she faltered. 'Our conversation the first day I came out here . . . '

He looked bemused. 'We covered quite a variety of subjects then.'

'When you mentioned Foxcovers' history. Your comment, how did you put it . . . ' She paused and frowned for effect. She knew exactly what he'd said. Word for word. And every one had twisted like a knife in her heart. But he wasn't to know that.

'Something about, 'my defence of a swindler'. I got the distinct impression you have no time for people who break the law.'

His eyes narrowed. 'Ah. Mr Lancaster again.' He nodded. 'Yes, I do remember. I also recall saying you were right to take the stance you did.' He raised a brow and she knew she had no argument. 'There's nothing wrong in having a passionate belief in someone when you have the whole picture, Megan.'

She swallowed, wishing fervently she'd not raised the subject again. But if ever the time was right to pour out her heart, it was now. Yet how could she share her past with him? Even if they were to meet again after the work at Foxcovers was complete, she could never enlighten him. She would still feel she had betrayed his trust in some way.

'You don't have to convince me about that,' she said softly.

He took his tone from her. 'I was wrong to be so flippant about something I know nothing about, but which obviously matters a lot to you and I'm sorry.' He gave her a wry look. 'Apology accepted?'

She managed a smile. 'Of course it is, but really there's no need for one.'

'I'd argue with that.' The warmth was back in his expression and for the second time in a matter of minutes, his concern was too much to handle.

She had to hide her feelings. She shook her head. 'I don't like arguments,' she said firmly. 'Tell me more about your work instead.'

'You're really interested?' Jordan threw her a smile. How could it be he felt he'd known her for far longer than a few days. He shook this thought aside and concentrated on what she'd just asked.

'Of course,' she nodded.

'Right.' He placed his mug on the

table and stretching his long legs out in front of him, scissored one across the other.

'As a barrister, I have the choice to work either for the defence or the prosecution. And I have prosecuted in the past when I've felt strongly enough about a particular case. But nine times out of ten I work for the defendant, not against.'

She still looked apologetic. 'It's my turn to say sorry. You make me feel like I've insulted you in some way.'

'Now you're being ridiculous,' he chastised gently. 'There'll always be the need for prosecuting counsel. Some of the people I admire most are on that side of the fence.' He shrugged. 'But if I sense a whiff of injustice, I'm like a dog with a bone.'

Why did hearing him say that matter so much? Why the lump in her throat? She swallowed against it. 'I hope your clients realise how lucky they are.'

He shrugged. 'It's my job. And talking of work, I still don't know how

115

you came to set up your business.'

Megan's heart flipped. Any further talk of her past and she could so easily say the wrong thing again.

She checked her watch. 'Sorry. No time for that now. I've a panelling expert due any moment. He's going to check how the handrails can be removed safely.'

'Sounds interesting,' Jordan smiled. He no sooner spoke than a loud rapping on the front door grabbed both their attention.

'That could be him now,' Megan said with a feeling of relief.

10

'This is a great place,' Jordan enthused, glancing around and taking Megan's attention away from the two grey squirrels who were watching them expectantly.

'Yes, it is, isn't it,' she agreed. 'In Norman times Delamere Forest was a royal hunting ground for the Earls of Chester.'

She turned back to the squirrels and tried to coax them nearer with some sandwich crusts. She had happily agreed to showing Jordan a little more of the local countryside when work stopped at the house for lunch, suggesting they pay a visit to the village sandwich bar first and insisting lunch was on her.

'Abbie would love it,' Jordan mused.

'That's what I was thinking.' She smiled. 'She could run round here for miles, burn off some of that energy of hers and still not see it all.'

'But you'll have to come back with us.'

Jordan hoped he sounded more casual than he was feeling. Each time they were together he realised Megan was coming to mean more to him.

'Maybe when the work's finished at the house,' she suggested, while her heart told her to tread carefully.

She turned her head to watch the squirrels leap to another tree and a shaft of sunlight turned her hair to shimmering gold.

Jordan caught his breath. Picking the bottled spring water he'd chosen when Megan had bought lunch, he took a pull from it. Wouldn't do, he told himself, to give her the slightest hint of the effect she was having on him.

He cleared his throat. 'To get back to our conversation before the panel man arrived . . . ' Megan's heart sank. ' . . . I'd love to hear how you got started with Time Savers.'

Abstractedly, she looped her hair behind her ears and warning herself to tread very carefully said, 'It was while I worked for a secretarial agency. One of our clients half-jokingly asked me if we covered domestic requirements, too. He was a busy executive, divorced, who just couldn't find the time for simple things like taking his suits to the dry cleaners, or keeping his kitchen cupboards stocked.'

'I know the feeling.' Jordan grimaced.

'Don't worry.' Megan grinned. 'You're not the only one. So,' she picked up again, 'that's when I saw the gap in the market and decided to try my luck with my own business. Jane, a lifelong friend, was keen to come in, too. At the beginning it was tough. We had no finances to speak of. Just a great idea and a lot of determination to see it through.'

Jordan frowned. 'You must have worked yourself into the ground if you had no funds at all.'

'There would have been if my adoptive great-aunt hadn't disinherited me and left all her assets to several animal charities. She was a little eccentric,' she added quickly.

'Sorry, I didn't mean to rake up bad memories.' Was this what she was holding back, he wondered.

Her eyes were shadowed, but steady. 'Don't concern yourself, Jordan,' she dismissed. 'I'm over it . . . well and truly. Starting off was also a lot of fun. The premises were originally a rundown hardware store which Jeff converted into offices for us. The upstairs storage rooms were turned into a flat.' She gave him a wry smile. 'Two for the price of one. I've lived there for almost three years. I've a business that takes up all my time and is growing nicely. So what more could I ask for?'

'So you're into empire building?'

Her brows shot up. 'An empire.' She laughed. 'As far as that goes, I'm strictly small fry.'

This time her laughter wasn't shared.

'Don't be modest, Megan,' he argued. 'You've come up with a brilliant idea.

Like you said, these days more people are living life in the fast lane; chasing a dream they think is the be all and end all.'

He gave her a grim look. 'As you continue to grow, you'll have business experts falling over themselves to give you advice. Yours is an original idea. You could have a worldwide franchise before you know it, and,' his eyes held hers, 'find yourself living the same life as your executive clients.'

Until he had walked into her life, nothing else but Time Savers had mattered. But now? The role of wife and mother shifted forward unexpectedly.

She chose her words carefully. 'I'd say that when you find the one thing that matters most, whether it be a life partner or a career, there's nothing wrong in allowing it to take over your existence.'

'At the expense of everything else?' Jordan challenged. 'How can you justify that? Surely a satisfying life is a combination of many things . . . many experiences.'

She was stumped and she knew it. She shrugged and chose the only line of defence she could think of . . . time, or more specifically, the lack of it. 'Jordan, I can't sit here discussing the merits of what comprises a happy life. There's work to be supervised back at your house. It's time we got back.'

'Ok, Megan. You win.' He picked up the plastic wrappings and other detritus from off the table and took them over to a nearby waste bin.

Megan watched, uncertain of his mood. Then as she walked back over to where she was standing, his smile brought with it a feeling of relief.

'Thanks for lunch,' he said. 'Pity we have to leave when it was getting really interesting. But you're right. For the time being, making Foxcovers habitable takes priority over everything else.'

Megan glanced up at his face. A face

imprinted in her mind every waking moment and during hours of troubled sleep. She gave him a wry smile. 'Well, that at least is one thing we're both agreed on.'

11

Standing in the centre of the empty drawing room, for the second time in a matter of minutes, Jordan went over the list of furniture he had in storage, and at Megan's suggestion tried to picture again the most effective arrangement.

But what did it matter now, he mused. This time tomorrow it would be here. It could be sorted then. And where, he wondered, had the last two weeks gone?

'It's no good,' he called over to her.

Megan paused midway from securing another hook in the gold and silver brocade drapes. 'What isn't?' She frowned.

'Trying to decide what goes where,' he complained. 'Forget it. I'll sort it tomorrow.' He shoved the list in his back pocket and came over to the ladder. 'Let me give you a hand. Those drapes look heavy.'

Megan didn't want to admit defeat, but her arms were beginning to feel like they were coming out of their sockets.

'Well, they are a lot heavier than I first thought.' She brushed away a lock of hair which had escaped from the scrunchie holding it back in a ponytail; along with the familiar niggle that it wasn't quite ethical to have Jordan do the work he was paying her to do.

He gave her an old fashioned look as he took the weight of them. 'Why didn't you say something instead of struggling on your own?'

'I thought I could manage. When I've finished these, I'll give Abbie's room a last once-over before her furniture arrives in the morning.'

'I can't believe it's all coming together,' Jordan said, 'and Abbie and I will be living here permanently.'

'I'm sure you're both going to be very happy at Foxcovers.' She turned away before he read the loss in her eyes, and got back to work.

Jordan watched Megan's fingers fly as she hooked the drapes on to the rail. Happy? Of course he'd be happy . . . of a kind. But true happiness? He was as far away from that than he'd ever been.

'Done.' Megan expelled a sigh from her efforts. 'Now there's just the one for the other side.'

She started down the steps, but her haste made them wobble. With a small yelp of fright, she tightened her hold. Jordan moved like greased lightning. One hand gripped the steps as he pushed against it. The other took hold of her waist like a vice.

Then the next moment she found herself carefully deposited on the floor.

'Thank you.' She took a long, steadying breath, avoiding his eyes. He would let her go in a minute and then she'd be fine.

But when his hands remained in place, expectation snatched that breath away again. Uncertainty made her tremble and caused him to misunderstand her feelings.

'Megan,' he gruffly reassured, tipping her chin with the lightest of touches so she had nowhere else to look but into the depths of his eyes. 'It's OK. You're safe now.'

Then he drew her closer and did what he'd wanted to do since the first moment he'd set eyes on her. He captured her lips and kissed her.

As her head swam, somewhere in the far distance a small voice warned she shouldn't be doing this. This was not what she wanted. This could lead to all kinds of complications.

She had to stop him. She really did. If only for the reason there were other people here. Any one of them could come looking for her. But as Jordan's kiss deepened and she responded, all thoughts of anything else were lost to the wonderful sensations his touch released.

Then it seemed her initial concern came back to mock her when a loud rapping on the door snatched them apart.

'Mr Alexander?' Jeff's muffled enquiry could just be heard outside in the hall.

'How's that for timing?' Jordan said huskily.

Megan gazed back at him, her senses still tingling.

'Megan?' The longing in his eyes was overwhelming. 'We have to talk.'

With Jordan momentarily distracted, she slipped behind him and tried desperately to focus on coming back down to earth.

'Mr Alexander?' Jeff repeated.

'Yes. In here, Jeff.' Jordan's voice couldn't have sounded more relaxed.

For a moment Megan remained rooted to the spot. While she appreciated his broad back screened her as she got on top of her feelings, she decided somewhat disgruntled, that men obviously had a faster recovery rate than women.

She picked up the drapes to check the hooks were in place. Wasn't his heart still beating ten to the dozen? Didn't his limbs feel like water?

She struggled to concentrate on fixing the hooks and considered going up the stepladder again. Could she make it to the top step of the tiny platform and risk a re-run of what had just happened?

'Just came to tell you the bathroom's finished,' she heard Jeff say.

Surprise got the upper hand. She turned and peered around Jordan. 'That was quick, Jeff.'

'Oh, hello, Megan. Didn't see you there. Yes, all the woodwork's done now the new fittings are in place.'

'I'll walk with you to the van, Jeff,' she heard him say. 'Oh, and Megan.' She broke off from eyeing up the ladder and glanced back at him. 'No more climbing until I get back,' he warned. 'Can't have you falling off again if I'm not here.' A teasing light in his eyes brought a little more colour to her cheeks.

The moment Jordan and Jeff disappeared around the door, she dragged the ladder over to the other side of the bay. After making doubly sure the foot was securely wedged, she picked up the drapes. Holding them over her arm, she gingerly took the first step. Then as her confidence in the ladder returned, she told herself she'd have the job done and dusted before Jordan came back.

'Don't you think so, Mr Lawrence?' As the two men made their way out of the house, Jeff's conversation finally registered in Jordan's preoccupation with Megan.

He frowned. He had no idea what he was supposed to give an opinion on. But then, not waiting for an answer, Jeff carried on talking ten to the dozen about the building trade.

It wasn't that he couldn't figure why he'd kissed her, he returned to his thoughts. The need had been growing for days.

But could he afford to run the risk of becoming emotionally involved with another ambitious woman?

Granted, as far as personalities went, Megan was a million miles from Claire.

But the way she had worked over the past weeks, making sure everything down to the last detail was perfection, had more than proved she was a woman whose dedication to her business was second to none.

Inside the drawing room Megan stepped back and admired the brocade drapes gracing the leaded casement windows and tinted glass. The silver and gold threads of the rich fabric picked up the light and looked absolutely perfect.

The pine wainscoting on all four walls was the perfect background for the precious few of her father's paintings she had, she reflected. The plain magnolia walls of her flat didn't really do them justice.

Paintings she had kept hidden from her great-aunt and uncle for the ten years she had lived with them, until the emotional day when at last she'd been able to proudly hang them in her own living room and bedroom.

She swallowed against the ache of

longing. A room like this was where they truly belonged. She bit her lip. If only . . .

She looked away. It was time to make herself scarce. She didn't want to be there when Jordan came back and saw she had ignored his wishes.

She touched her lips tenderly, his swift capture of them still a sweet memory, then brought herself back down to earth. It was just a kiss. One kiss. That was all.

Dashing her misery away, she braced herself to cope with carrying the weight of the ladders down to the far end of the corridor.

That done she hurried upstairs. In one sense, she was pleased how everything had progressed so smoothly. But the sting was that tomorrow Jordan and Abbie would be settled in and her work here would be over until September.

Six weeks without seeing him again. Maybe it was for the best. Viewed from a distance, she was bound to see things in a different light and once and for all put an end to wishful thinking.

Outside on the drive, Jordan shook hands with Jeff. 'Appreciate what you've done, Jeff. And thanks again for re-jigging your schedule with Megan so I could be in by the weekend. It matters . . . matters a lot.'

Jeff brushed aside his thanks. 'No problem at all. Truth be known, I've got a soft spot for the lass. Can't have been easy starting up from scratch; working well into the night to make a go of her business. Which she still does, so I'm told, even though she doesn't have to. I keep telling her slow down, make some time for yourself not everybody else. But she just laughs and says I haven't got it. That's what her work is all about.'

Jordan glanced back towards the house. 'True enough,' he said soberly.

'Well, it seems such a waste to me,' Jeff continued, as they both waited while two of his men packed the last items of equipment into the van.

'Young woman like that should be dangling babies on her knee and keeping some man happy.'

'Don't let her hear you say that,' Jordan exclaimed with some humour. And yet, hadn't he been thinking along the same lines himself. 'I want you back to finish the rest of the house.'

Jeff dismissed Jordan's concerns with a shrug. 'Oh, she knows what I think. I tell her often enough. And d'you know,' he added on a more serious note as the men finally finished loading and climbed inside, 'even though she's too polite to give me a mouthful, and says that will never happen,' he tapped the side of his nose with his finger, 'I get the feeling there's nothing she'd like better.'

As he went back inside, Jordan reflected on what Jeff had just said. Had he really got it right about Megan wanting to be a wife and mother.

Jeff was right. It was a terrible waste. She was a natural with children. Her easy, friendly manner with Abbie; the way the child flowered in her company was evidence of that.

Inside the empty drawing room, the sight of both curtains hanging neatly at the window, Megan and the stepladder gone, had him frowning. She wouldn't dream of it, would she?

Under his breath he cursed her independence. If the ladders had tilted again and she'd been alone . . .

Damn it, it was his house. He was employing her. If he felt like helping out, she should just grin and bear it, instead of constantly showing that independent side of her nature.

Now where was she? Most likely place? Something was telling him Abbie's room.

12

As Jordan reached the open doorway he saw Megan standing in front of the window with her back to him, looking out.

He could tell by her posture she was deep in thought. 'Why didn't you wait and let me give you a hand with the other curtain? If the ladders had overbalanced again . . . '

His terse words made her tense. He saw the effect and frowned. He hadn't meant to sound so churlish.

She kept her back to him. 'I made doubly sure they couldn't.'

'When everyone else is giving their all,' he attempted to explain his anger, 'lending a hand makes me feel less of a spare part.'

There was a long moment before she turned to acknowledge his admission and when she did, the confirmation of what he'd been thinking was there, written all over her face. She was embarrassed about what had happened in the drawing-room.

It was like a slap across the face. So he had been kidding himself when he'd felt her sweet response. He cleared his throat. 'Anyway, they look perfect.'

'I'm pleased you're satisfied,' she said a little stiffly.

The formality he'd greeted her with the day they'd first met was back. And could she blame him? She felt instantly deflated. Jordan was obviously deeply regretting their kiss.

He cleared his throat. 'You've done a fantastic job. I'm forever indebted to you.'

There he went again. Indebted. That sounded so clinical. Well, that was all right. In fact, it was just what she needed if she was to stand any chance of living some kind of normal life knowing now what it was like to have been kissed by him.

'Indebted?' She gave him a wry

smile. 'I don't expect that.' She shrugged. 'It's my job . . . what I do. But if you're that pleased, you could always put your comments down on paper and I'll add it to the folio of satisfied clients.'

Satisfied client. So that was him in a nutshell. He raked a hand through his hair and still couldn't stop himself from saying, 'And there was I, conceited enough to think this contract was a little bit special.'

A frown flitted across her brow. Her troubled eyes searched his face for some clue to what he was thinking, but his expression gave nothing away. He meant the work on the house, of course, she concluded.

'I doubt there's a conceited bone in your body,' she argued. 'But it's true. This contract was . . . is special. And meeting Abbie was a joy.'

The house, his daughter. What about him? He decided to go for it. Raising an eyebrow he asked, 'And her father?'

For a moment she looked flustered

and pink cheeked. But the vulnerability in her eyes gave him hope. 'Her father has proved . . . interesting.'

He searched her face. 'Can I take that as a compliment?'

'You can take it any way you want.' Her half-smile increased his optimism.

'In that case, I'll go for the positive and assume you've enjoyed my company.'

'Of course I have.' She folded her arms against her T-shirt and gave him a wry smile. 'For most of the time,' she added just in case her admission went straight to his head.

'Well, that's put me in my place,' he said dryly. 'But I have to tell you your ordeal's not over yet.'

She swallowed. 'It isn't?' He wasn't to know each day she kept her secrets from him was becoming just that.

'If I have my way, not by a long chalk. I'm more than certain I'm going to have to call on your help again next week while Abbie and I are settling in. You can do that, can't you?'

How could she resist? But she wasn't going to let him think one word from him and she'd coming running. 'Right now, I can't say. Who knows what Jane's put me down for.'

His expression of overdone disappointment had her smiling and the tension they had both been feeling was broken. 'I'll confirm with you later.'

She looked around for some much-needed distraction and decided to give the pink curtains a final tweak. 'You're pleased with Abbie's room?' she called over her shoulder.

'More than.' Here again she'd worked wonders with his daughter. Making out she had all the time in the world for her while, with a little gentle guidance, had had Abbie believing the wallpaper now brightening the room with its tiny floral print, pink of course, on a white background had been her choice alone. 'She loves it.'

And tomorrow the pine furniture would be in place on the apple green carpet, and Abbie would have the home she deserved. 'There will be some excitement here tomorrow night, believe me,' he said.

Megan turned and faced him again. 'Is Abbie coming out with you in the morning?'

'Not first thing. She's spending the day at Jenny's until everything's in place. I'll pick her up after that and bring her home.'

Bring her home. How much his words had touched her. 'I'd love to see her face when she sees her room.' Her thoughts were out in the open before she realised. Instantly she regretted it. Tomorrow was for Jordan and Abbie . . . and more than likely, Diane, too.

He grabbed the opportunity. 'We're banking on it. She'll expect you here. Just as I do,' he added after a moment's pause.

Did he really mean it, or was he just being polite? 'Abbie said that?'

'On a regular basis this last week. She's also got it in her head that you'll join us for our first meal at Foxcovers.

She has it all planned.'

'She has?'

He nodded. 'Right down to the family-sized pizza she's given me strict instructions to order. But don't feel obliged.' He scratched the side of his head. 'It's such short notice. You must have something more intersting planned than Saturday night in with a widower, his seven-year-old daughter and a take-away pizza. I'll explain to Abbie we should have asked you sooner. She'll understand.'

'Don't do that,' she said softly.

What Jordan had just described was the most attractive proposition she'd heard in a long time. 'If Abbie wants me here, of course I'll come.'

He seemed relieved. For his daughter's sake, of course, she reckoned. 'If the weather holds we could take the camping table and chairs out on to the terrace,' she suggested. 'It will be lovely with the sun around the back of the house. I'll make up a salad to go with it and some dips. Oh, and what about a celebration cake?'

There she went again, Jordan marvelled. Taking an idea and expanding it into something better. He could just imagine Abbie's delight at her suggestion. 'I'll tell her this evening when I pick her up, and thanks, Megan.'

'None needed.' She smiled. 'It's been a triumph for Time Savers and a pleasure.'

'Likewise Miss Moore, if you have your company hat on.'

His formal expression made her chuckle. 'Honestly, Jordan, I feel very flattered by what you've been saying.'

He shook his head. 'Flattery had nothing to do with it. I'm a good judge of character. After our first meeting everything told me you were someone who delivered, and you've more than proved that. If there's one thing I despise, it's a liar. No matter what the situation, there's no excuse for deceit.'

The stark emphasis of his words chilled her heart and seemed to change the whole atmosphere of the room. She drew a breath to combat the devastation of what she was feeling. This really was the end.

To combat her despair, she changed the subject. 'I'd best get down to the kitchen. The team should be just about finished by now.'

A little later, Jordan watched from inside the porch until Megan's Volvo turned out of the drive, then with a preoccupied air went back inside.

Starting on the ground floor he contrasted the rooms that had been transformed to those yet to be worked on.

Come Christmas he should have a house . . . a home to be justly proud of. At the very top of the house, the lingering traces of oil paint brought back the memory of Megan's defence of Gideon Lancaster. Maybe he could do something for her in return.

He took out his mobile and pressed the office number. 'Diane? Yes, everything's gone really well. Couldn't be better. The reason I'm ringing . . . '

After dropping off her team of domestics at their respective addresses, Megan headed back for the office. When she got back she would have to tell Jane she wouldn't be able to make it tomorrow night.

She frowned. Jane would run the gamut of emotions. Disappointment because she would be turning down yet another social engagement, curiosity when she knew the reason why, and concern if she gained the slightest indication of how much her feelings for Jordan were getting out of hand.

13

When Megan saw the front door open and Abbie come racing out to greet her, the impact of how much she'd miss seeing her hit hard.

Determined not to ruin these last few hours they would spend together, she quickly got out of her car and was almost knocked off her feet by the child's over-excited greeting.

Megan led her around to the back of the car and unlocked the boot. 'You can help me carry the salad and dips in.'

'Need another pair of hands?'

Megan looked up. Jordan was coming across the drive. Against his white open-necked shirt, his skin glowed with life and everything wonderfully masculine she could think of.

'Here, Dad, you take this.' Abbie handed him the biggest container. 'I'll take the other one and Megan can have the smallest 'cos you said she hasn't stopped working all day. Have you ordered the pizza?'

'Done the minute you said Megan was here,' he confirmed with a grin. They both watched as Abbie charged off towards the house, box in hand. 'I won't be surprised if today's excitement becomes all too much for her,' Jordan added, 'and she'll crash out not long after we've eaten.'

Megan closed the boot. 'She's happy with her room?'

'Ecstatic. Be prepared to spend half the evening up there.'

Megan chuckled. 'I don't mind.'

Jordan threw her a look that doubled her heart rate. 'But I do.'

She fought to overcome this and asked, 'And Diane, is she here?'

Jordan's frown was unexpected. 'Diane?' he echoed. 'Never entered my head. I imagine she'll have far more exciting things planned with Chris . . . especially now. Although, maybe it would have been nice for us all to meet up.'

'Chris?' Megan had to ask.

'Her boyfriend. No, actually, her fiancé, she told me about her engagement when I spoke to her yesterday afternoon. Chris works abroad a lot and popped the question when he got back the night before last. Now wait a minute.' Jordan took one look at Megan's expression and began to laugh. 'You thought . . . No. It's my fault. I should have explained the day I brought Diane round to see the house. She's my secretary, Megan. Coming up to four years now and goodness knows how I'd function if she wasn't there to keep me organised.'

His secretary! A bubble of happiness burst inside. 'Oh, I see.' She smiled. 'Sorry.'

Jordan gave her a quizzical look. 'Nothing to apologise for. Come on, we'd best go inside.'

Later, Jordan pushed his empty plate away with a satisfied sigh. 'I can't remember when I've enjoyed a meal at home so much.'

He glanced across the table where Abbie was struggling to stay awake. 'Can you, kitten?'

Elbow on the table, head resting in one hand, Abbie muttered something indecipherable.

Jordan and Megan exchanged looks. 'I think it's time I took my daughter to bed, don't you?'

With that, Abbie blinked her eyes open. 'I want Megan to come, too.'

Her father's eyes sought the heavens before passing Megan a wry look. 'D'you mind?'

'Of course not.' She shook her head at his reactions and got to her feet. 'Come on, Abbie. Let me see that great room of yours again.'

With Abbie asleep almost as soon as her head touched the pillow, Jordan and Megan made their way downstairs.

'Thanks for this evening,' she said after she had helped him clear the table and bring the dishes inside.

He paused from filling the dishwasher. 'That sounds like you're leaving. You can't go, not yet.'

'It's getting late,' she protested, while her heart said, I don't want this to end either.

'Stay. Have a nightcap,' he insisted, reaching for the cafetiere. 'Curl up in one of the chairs and relax. Besides, if this is going to be the last time I see you until you can fit us in again, you have to indulge me. Go on now,' he gestured with his eyes, 'or I'll pick you up and carry you over.'

She chuckled as she went over to the two fat armchairs she'd decided earlier that day would look perfect to both sides of the now-gleaming range.

She sank down into the cream depths of one of them and made herself comfortable. It was now or never. The initial euphoria of knowing Jordan had no-one in his life had been replaced by the certainty that after what he'd said about deception, she would never be the one to take that place. 'It could be a lot longer than I'd anticipated,' she announced.

He stopped pouring and frowned. 'Longer? Coming here, you mean?'

Would she be cursed more than she already was for telling white lies? Probably. If not, she deserved it.

'The reason I didn't get round to calling you back this afternoon,' she began, 'was the amount of work booked in for the coming weeks. It took some sorting through.'

He gazed at her moodily. 'I see.'

'Things have been piling up . . . ' she made the excuse.

He brought two mugs over and handed one to her before taking the other chair. 'Tell me about it.' There was a stiffness in his response. 'That's why I took stock of my life some months back; saw what really was important . . . like watching my daughter growing up.'

'You're blessed to have that distraction,' she said without rancour. 'I'm not that lucky. But I have some idea of the

151

pain you went through when you lost your wife. Abbie must make up for it.'

'Pain!' The bitterness of his retort startled her. She watched with uncertain eyes while he placed his mug down on the floor. When he looked back up at her, it was with raw emotion. He sat forward on the edge of the chair and linked his fingers together, for a moment lost in thought.

'The pain was there long before the accident, Megan. In a broken marriage, the hurt a small child went through from the actions of her mother who became bored very quickly with the idea of looking after a child.'

Megan's eyes widened, disbelieving of what she was hearing. 'Jordan, I had no idea — '

'Of course you didn't.' His interruption was curt. 'No-one did. Claire was very good at playing the correct role perfectly when she thought it necessary. But even that became a chore. No wonder that precious child of mine was confused at times.'

Silence hung heavily for a few moments, then Megan asked quietly, 'The crash. It happened two years ago to the day, didn't it?'

He shook his head. 'No. It was on the night of the twenty-eighth when the accident happened. Thankfully that was one blazing row Abbie did not witness. I've handled enough guilt over the ones she did hear. It was traumatic enough for her to learn her mother had died. For her last memory to have been one of Claire screeching like an alley cat would have been unbearable.

'As it was, Abbie was withdrawn for months. Claire left that night with someone she'd been having an affair with. They were flying out to the States where, apparently, he was poised to hit the big time with one of the major law firms. And while I despised her for leaving her child, there was no way she was taking her from me.'

His eyes glinted. 'They obviously couldn't wait to start the celebrations. They'd both been drinking.'

Megan could barely take in Jordan's revelations. She cleared her throat. 'Claire wasn't the one — '

'Behind the wheel.' He shook his head. 'They were in her car, but it was Richard who was driving.'

There was another long pause then Jordan remembered his coffee and picked up the mug. He took a few sips then said, 'Moving here on the twenty-ninth, after the second anniversary, was symbolic of the new start I desperately needed for myself and Abbie. A new life for us both.'

'I'm sorry,' Megan said. 'I shouldn't have drawn those conclusions . . . even raised the subject.'

'No. It's fine.' His features relaxed again. 'Foxcovers is having a therapeutic effect already. Then again,' his eyes lightened, 'it could be down to a sympathetic ear. Either way it's a good feeling to finally get the mockery of my marriage off my chest. I'd recommend it. And if you ever need a shoulder to cry on, I'm your man.'

★ ★ ★

Alone in her office, well after Jane and Stephanie had left for the day, Megan finished typing up the last notes for the Foxcovers' contract. Her mood was just as sombre as when she'd left Jordan on Saturday night.

The image of him revealing the truth of his marriage remained clear in her mind. And while she was flattered he should want to bare his soul to her, the guilt was ever present that she still could not bring herself to reveal her past to him.

She sighed softly and got up from her desk to file the papers away. Inside the folder she saw the envelope containing the house keys she had forgotten to give back.

She picked it up, reflected for a moment then came to a decision. Taking the keys back to Jordan would serve a purpose. She owed it to him to be just as open about her past as he had been over his failed marriage and the loss of his wife.

She dropped them into her bag. Besides, once he knew she was Gideon Lancaster's daughter, she would no longer have any need of them.

'This is something of a surprise after what you said on Saturday,' Jordan said when he opened the front door to see Megan standing there. 'Come in.'

She hesitated. This was going to be a thousand times harder than she'd imagined. She ignored his invitation. Outside was much better for what she had to say. She could take to her heels as soon as she saw the inevitable contempt he was bound to feel.

She shook her head. 'I was just passing. I . . . the keys,' she floundered, offering them to him. 'I forgot to let you have them back.' She tried a smile but it didn't work.

He gave her a guarded look before saying, 'But you'll need them when the work starts again in September.'

This conversation was not going as

she'd planned. She swallowed. 'September's a long way off. A lot could happen in between.'

'Like what?' he pounced with a marked frown. 'No. Before you come up with whatever reason you have for your boredom with me, you can come inside and tell me. I don't do doorstep conversations.'

Boredom!

As she watched him turn away and walk down the hall and read the tension in his shoulders, she found herself aching to reassure him that he couldn't be more wrong.

She owed him the truth. On weakened legs she followed him inside and quietly closed the front door.

When she reached the kitchen he was standing in front of the table, opening a large envelope. A scattering of what looked like house-warming cards and correspondence lay in front of him.

So he was giving out signals that what she had to say didn't matter that much anyway. She prayed she was right.

She made an attempt to ease the tension filling the room. 'Where's Abbie today?'

'Up in her room, reading. We spent the day in Llandudno. Not long back.'

He pulled out a sheaf of papers, his interest momentarily taken, then he threw her a glance. 'Can I get you a drink?'

'No, thank you.' Her voice had an edge to it. All right, so he was mad at her for what he considered as being let down, but there was no need for this ice-cold attitude. 'I can't stay long.'

'Of course you can't,' he agreed, his tone patronising. 'You're a woman with a highly successful business to run. You mustn't waste your time here when you have so many other clients desperate for attention.'

'Jordan, that's unfair.' This wasn't going to work. There was no point in staying a minute longer she decided as Jordan looked back at the papers Diane had sent and flicked the top one over.

'I'd better go.' She placed the keys on

the table and turned to leave.

'Perhaps you should . . . Miss Lancaster.' From across the room his bitter words hit like a physical blow.

She placed her hand on the kitchen table for support before turning back to him, dreading what she would meet in his eyes.

'You've been lying from the start.' His voice was full of quiet contempt. 'Taking me for some kind of idiot.' He flung the papers down on the table in front of her. Amongst the scattered sheets, a photocopied picture of her parents looked up at her; her mother's features, so like her own, confirming all she'd kept back from him.

'From the word go, every exchange we had was a sham.' His increasing disdain brought more volume to his tone.

'Jordan, please listen — '

'Why? So you can fool me with more lies?' He demanded over her words.

'I've never lied to you,' she defended hotly. 'You must let me explain.'

'Must I?' The ice in his tone chilled her.

'It's the reason I called here today,' she explained, refusing to be put off by his anger. 'As I got to know you and Abbie better, the guilt of keeping my family history from you became unbearable. I owe you an explanation . . . I know that. Yes, I am guilty of keeping things from you, but not of lying to you.'

'It comes a pretty close second,' he thundered.

'Jordan, please — '

'Stop it!' The cry of anguish from the doorway turned Megan's blood cold. Horror-stricken, she turned quickly to see Abbie standing there, her face contorted, her small body trembling. 'You're making my dad shout just like Mummy did. I thought you were my friend, but you're not.'

Megan started towards her. 'Abbie, I am your friend, you and your dad mean everything to me.'

'No, we don't. If you loved us you

160

wouldn't make him shout.'

'Abbie.' From behind her, Megan heard the pain in Jordan's voice.

Ignoring her father, Abbie spun around and slammed the door shut behind her.

'Jordan,' Megan pleaded as he rushed past her, 'you must let me — '

'Leave us,' he demanded in a voice she didn't recognise. 'You've done enough damage for one day.'

In something of a daze Megan walked back to her car. Sitting there for a moment, she dashed the tears away from her face before turning on the ignition. Then with trembling hands she gripped the steering wheel and eased the car down the drive.

As she drove back to the village she tried to find some consolation in knowing the truth was out, but her heart was heavy, her limbs felt like lead and she felt chilled to the bone.

And Abbie? That sweet little child. How was she going to live with the hurt she'd cause her?

14

The ringing of Megan's doorbell shattered the troubled sleep she had fallen into.

Thoughts of Jordan and Abbie returned immediately as she uncurled herself on the sofa. She frowned as the ringing sounded again and kept on sounding.

Hastily, she released the catch and opened the door. She was thrown to see the back of Jordan's tense figure in front of her, head down, his finger still pressed on the bell.

'Jordan?' At the sound of her voice he spun around.

She was shocked by his appearance. Anguish was carved in his face; his complexion almost the same shade of grey as his frantic eyes. She quickly looked through the gap between his shoulder and the door frame towards the kerb where his vehicle was parked, expecting to see Abbie. But she was not there.

She frowned. Surely he hadn't left her at home alone. Not after all she'd been through earlier?

'Where's — '

'Tell me she's here.' His raw demand crushed her concern as he pushed his way inside.

Then the hairs on the back of her neck prickled when the implication of what he was saying hit home. She gripped the edge of the door for support; the horror of the situation making her feel nauseous. 'Jordan, you can't mean . . . Abbie's missing!'

'Don't tell me she isn't here.'

'But how could she be?' she reasoned, not daring to think Abbie might have stopped a passing car. 'It's almost five miles to the village. I haven't seen Abbie since I left you.'

His body seemed to buckle. 'I'll have to phone the police.'

She reached out to support him.

'Jordan, are you sure you've made a thorough search? Abbie wouldn't leave the house or the grounds; not on her own. She's small, but not irresponsible.'

'Irresponsible, no. But after what she overheard this afternoon, who can tell what she'd do?'

The accusation in his eyes brought Megan's hand to her mouth. Did he have to be so cutting?

'It took some time for me to settle her down after you'd gone. She was physically shattered and wouldn't stop crying.'

Megan stared at him white-faced.

'I thought rest the best thing for her. I stayed with her until she fell asleep and went back up to her room later to see how she was. Her bed was empty. I checked the house, the gardens.' He raked a frantic hand through his hair.

Megan's mind raced over any possibility, then she rallied. Her heart skipped a beat as she thought of a possibility. 'Jordan,' she exclaimed, 'I've an idea. Give me a moment. I'll just get my keys.'

He followed her up the stairs. 'Megan, I need to phone the police!'

'Trust me, Jordan,' she called as she hurried over to pick up her bag. 'Abbie was very curious about a door in the grounds the first time you brought her to see the house. Remember, I took her exploring while you were busy with Jeff.'

His look of bewilderment told her he was in no fit state to think rationally. 'A door? Leading to where?'

She grabbed her bag and pushed him forward out of the room. 'A walled garden and a summerhouse,' she explained as she hurried after him down the stairs. 'She could be there.'

She took a breath, not wanting to consider the alternatives if she was wrong and unable to add, if there's still no sign of her, we'll have to contact the authorities.

Before Jordan had switched off the ignition, Megan was out of his vehicle and running around to the back of the house.

From the heavy rustling sounds behind her, she knew he was fighting his way through the tangle of shrubs just as mindlessly as she was doing.

When she almost fell out on to the overgrown path that led to the walled garden, she heard him call after her, 'Megan, I've checked all around here. We're just wasting time.'

'We have to try,' she insisted. 'Look, the door's just here. She pointed over to the bramble thicket and the barely-visible door behind it. Her heart sank. It didn't look as if it had been disturbed since Abbie had first asked to see what was on the other side. 'We'll have to push our way through.'

Jordan frowned. 'But surely that door leads outside the property.'

She shook her head. With a riot of overgrown shrubs disguising a good part of the layout, it was an easy mistake to make. 'No, Jordan, it doesn't. Abbie and I were going to ask you about cutting the brambles down so we could get through, but then it was forgotten when we went for lunch. It's worth a try.'

The spark of hope in his eyes brought a lump to her throat and it hit her hard just how much she loved him. Please, she had to be right. She started forward.

'Hold on. Those brambles look lethal.' He manoeuvred himself in front of her. 'I'll go first.'

Regardless of the thorns, he pushed on around the thicket, taking care to hold the most vicious shoots to one side as Megan followed carefully after.

'Plenty wide enough for a child,' he said in hope, when they reached the door and he'd struggled to push it back as far as it would go. She followed after him and noticed he'd not escaped unscathed from his efforts. The blood-ied scratches on his arm and hands would need to be bathed later.

For a moment they stood in tense silence in the evening light and regarded the scene before them.

The only hint that this piece of land had ever been touched by man, was the faded blue wooden structure against the furthest wall, partially hidden by scrub oak saplings and tender young birch. Nature had truly taken over, Megan considered. The garden she remembered no longer existed.

Then her heart leapt. 'Jordan. Look there.' She pointed to the bent stems of scarlet poppies and white daisies brightening the carpet of wild grasses. They showed a regular track of evident disturbance. 'Someone's been through here. She could be in the summer-house.'

Before the possibility left her lips, Jordan took off. This time the wild flowers didn't stand a chance.

Megan held back. Half in desperate fear of her idea being proved wrong. Another part of her saying Jordan's reconciliation with his daughter was for him alone.

She held her breath as she watched

him disappear inside. Releasing it in a wave of relief when the sound of his triumphant call shattered the silence.

She took a step forward, then another until she was running on down through the knee-high grasses, tears of happiness running down her cheeks.

The sight of Jordan coming back outside with Abbie held firmly in the protection of his arms had her wiping her tears away.

She slowed down. She couldn't let them know how much they mattered to her.

'She was asleep.' His voice was gruff; little more than a whisper. 'You were right.'

Megan nodded, still fighting to stay in control of her emotions. She cleared her throat and gently said, 'So you found what was behind the old door after all, Abbie.'

Abbie lifted a sleepy head from Jordan's shoulder and sniffed. 'I was sad when Dad said we mightn't see you any more. I remembered the first time you took me round the garden, so I came outside while he was going through his papers. I saw the bushes you were worried I might hurt myself on. But I got round all right.'

'Oh, sweetheart.' Megan reached up and stroked her arm.

She felt Jordan's eyes upon her and looked up to meet them and dared to hope what she saw there was love. She dragged her eyes from his back to Abbie. 'I felt very sad, too. But I knew in my heart I'd see you again.'

And when the child reached for her hand, it dawned on her that she had no idea of the worry she'd caused.

Doubt flickered across Abbie's face. 'But you made Dad shout again.'

'It wasn't Megan's fault, Abbie,' Jordan said. 'It was mine and I'm sorry. There's be no more shouting again . . . ever.' He ruffled her curls and looked up at Megan. His expression caused her heart to soar. 'That's right, isn't it, Megan,' he added, his tone softening.

She swallowed. 'That's right,' she echoed in little more than a whisper.

'Good,' Abbie exclaimed. 'I'm going to pick some flowers for Megan then to show you're sorry.'

Jordan managed a smile. 'Great idea. But promise me one thing.'

'What's that, Dad?'

'You will never ever go exploring again without asking me first.'

'I promise.'

Megan found she was still having some difficulty coping with the situation, when Jordan turned away from his daughter and gave her a lop-sided smile. 'Wild flowers preferable to a dozen red roses for the woman who means more than life to me?'

Hearing his words, Megan almost crumpled. Then it was wonderful to feel his arm around her shoulders. 'Every time,' she answered huskily, looking up at him.

She blinked back a fresh wave of tears. 'But I really am to blame for what happened,' she insisted shakily. 'I

171

should have told you right at the beginning what my connections to Foxcovers were. But the need to be involved with my old home, the fear that possibility would be snatched away again once you knew the circumstances of my background — '

He raised his hand and placed two fingers against her lips. His smile was that of a man who knew his love was returned without question. 'After what I've just told Abbie, we're not going to argue.'

She reached up and took his free hand, to have hers gripped firmly. He pulled her to him and feathered her lips with gentle kisses. Then he raised his head and gave her a wry smile. 'Is there any chance of you considering taking on a man and his child on a permanent basis?'

She raised her brows in mock surprise. 'After what you put me through today?' She made him wait for the answer he knew was coming. 'Definitely.'

'Megan, is it too much to ask you about your childhood?' Jordan asked after supper and Abbie was in bed. 'I'll understand if you find it too much of an ordeal.'

They were sitting close together on the sofa in the drawing-room. Jordan had the papers Diane had sent him alongside him, but he wanted to hear Megan's story from her own lips.

'Of course it isn't,' she insisted. 'You opened your heart to me about your marriage. And there's no-one else I'd rather tell what happened to my family.'

She then began to relate the memories he sensed still scarred. She told him of her mother's terminal illness and later learning of her father's desperate efforts to meet the cost of the private medical treatment he hoped would save her life.

The unhappiness of having to leave Foxcovers under the pretence of taking a holiday with her mother's aunt and uncle.

The one memory, Jordan noticed, which brought a wistful expression to the face he adored, was when Megan spoke of the unframed paintings she'd helped her father hide inside her suitcases the evening she was collected by her relatives. Portraits of herself and her mother and a series of Foxcovers' grounds in all four seasons. Paintings she would treasure for the rest of her life.

'Even though I was only eight years old at the time,' she threw him a wobbly smile, 'or eight and a quarter as Abbie would say, I remember Dad's last words, like they were spoken yesterday. 'They're our secret, Megs,' he said. I was warned never to let Constance or Henry see them because, in his words again, they didn't like him very much at the moment and he was afraid they would take them from me and they'd be destroyed. Of course I had no idea why. But I promised to keep them safe until I thought I would see both my parents again.

'The mystery of how anyone could dislike my father with such a passion was made clear before we'd exited the drive. Constance left me in no doubt that she laid the blame for my mother's illness squarely on dad's shoulders. And then,' her voice wavered.

Jordan placed his arm around her, saying nothing until she was ready to go on. ' . . . when we heard a few days later, that Mum had died. Well,' she grimaced, 'you can imagine how Constance took it. After that she spared me no details of the 'wickedness of that man'.

'I know it came as a shock to them both when Dad had his heart attack, but they didn't let me forget the prison sentence and criminal record he'd escaped by dying before the case came to trial. After that they legally adopted me purely for the reason of never wanting to hear the Lancaster name again.

'I intend having it changed back by deed poll, but building the business seems to have taken over everything else.' She gave him a half-smile. 'I'll get round to it very soon.

'The imposition of caring for me for the next ten years was made crystal clear. That's when Dad's paintings became even more precious to me.'

Listening in simmering anger of the appalling treatment Megan had received, Jordan felt he could take no more. 'Megan, I think that's enough. I don't want you torturing yourself by going over this for my sake,' he protested.

'For goodness sake, you were the same age as Abbie when you had all that to deal with. And then to rub salt in the wounds, I come along and ask you to renovate the house for me. It must have been a nightmare dealing with the irony. And why didn't you tell me at the beginning about your connections. It wouldn't have made any difference.' His love for her tightened his grip around her. 'I'd have still wanted you here.'

'But it wasn't a nightmare, Jordan,' Megan responded with feeling. 'It turned out to be the most wonderful thing that could have happened. I know you and Abbie will come to love the house as much as I do.'

'And you do have it back, you realise.' The unspoken significance of his words almost broke her composure.

When he brushed her mouth with his lips in a gesture of comfort, the reminder of her dreams of a man who would always be there for her, brought an added sheen to her eyes.

Then Jordan took his arm from around her shoulder and shifted position. 'Now let me read up on what was written at the time of your father's case. Then I'll let you know as far as the law goes, what I already imagine would have been the outcome had he stood trial.'

While Jordan studied the printed copies of the reports, Megan sat in contented silence, drinking in the features of the man who was her whole world.

After a matter of moments he reached for her hand and gave it an affectionate squeeze. Then he looked up. His smile warmed her heart. 'It's what I expected. Your father had every chance of being given a non-custodial sentence. It's a tragedy he didn't live to hear that verdict.'

While Jordan's revelations lifted a huge weight from her shoulders, the sadness remained. 'That's a wonderful consolation. Thank you.'

She gave him a wistful look. 'But had he lived, I don't think he could ever have coped with the shame of his actions. The realisation that no amount of private treatment from people who were at the very top of the medical profession, could have saved my mother would have been very hard for him to bear. And the loss of his precious Foxcovers to cover the debt he was in, I think would have finished him.'

She lapsed into silence as the

memories stirred, unaware Jordan had placed the papers to one side.

'Come here,' he instructed softly. She mustered a sad smile. 'He'd have still seen the beauty of his wife in his daughter, still had her love and believe me the unquestioning love of a child is priceless. Almost as precious,' he murmured as he took her in his arms again, 'as the true love of one's life. Welcome home, Megan.'

THE END

We do hope that you have enjoyed reading this large print book.

Did you know that all of our titles are available for purchase?

We publish a wide range of high quality large print books including:
**Romances, Mysteries, Classics
General Fiction
Non Fiction and Westerns**

Special interest titles available in large print are:
**The Little Oxford Dictionary
Music Book, Song Book
Hymn Book, Service Book**

Also available from us courtesy of Oxford University Press:
**Young Readers' Dictionary
(large print edition)
Young Readers' Thesaurus
(large print edition)**

For further information or a free brochure, please contact us at:
**Ulverscroft Large Print Books Ltd.,
The Green, Bradgate Road, Anstey,
Leicester, LE7 7FU, England.
Tel:** (00 44) 0116 236 4325
Fax: (00 44) 0116 234 0205

Other titles in the
Linford Romance Library:

SEASONS OF CHANGE

Margaret McDonagh

When Kathleen Fitzgerald left Ireland twenty years ago, she never planned to return. In England she married firefighter Daniel Jackson and settled down to raise their family. However, when Dan is injured in the line of duty, events have a ripple effect, bringing challenges and new directions to the lives of Dan, Kathleen and their children, as well as Kathleen's parents and her brother, Stephen. How will the members of this extended family cope with their season of change?

CHERRY BLOSSOM LOVE

Maysie Greig

Beth was in love with her boss, but he could only dream of the brief passionate interlude he had shared with a Japanese girl long ago, and of the child he had never seen. Beth agrees to accompany him to Japan in search of his daughter. There perhaps, the ghost of Madame Butterfly would be laid, and he would turn to her for solace . . . Her loyal heart is lead along dark and dangerous paths before finding the love she craves.

THE SEABRIGHT SHADOWS

Valerie Holmes

Elizabeth, bound to a marriage she wants no part in, is strong willed and determined to free herself from the arrangement her father Silas has made. But she is trapped. The family's fortunes are linked to and dependent upon her marriage to Mr Timothy Granger, a man she despises. It takes a bold act of courage and the interference of her Aunt Jessica to make her see the future in a different light and save the family from ruin.

THE TWO OF US

Jennifer Ames

When Mark Dexter, visiting Australia, invited Janet to work in his publishing house in the United States, she thought he was offering her heaven. They had an adventurous and thrilling trip by plane to New York, lingering in Fiji and Havana; but when they reached New York Janet found she could not get away from Julian Gaden, an odd character whom Mark had introduced her to in a Sydney night club . . .

JANIE

Iain Torr

Janie is a champion skier. Young and beautiful, she is continually in the news, while Roy is a struggling writer, obscure and lonely. He falls in love with her, but realises that she is far above him. Then, abruptly, the situation changes. Janie suffers an accident and slips out of the news, but Roy makes the headlines when the film rights of one of his books are sold . . . Can Janie and Roy overcome their differences and find lasting happiness?

PHOENIX IN THE ASHES

Georgina Ferrand

Paul Varonne had been dead for six months, yet at Château Varonne reminders of him were still evident. Living there was his mother, who still believed him alive and Chantal, his amoral cousin. Into this brooding atmosphere comes Paul's widow, Francesca, after a nervous breakdown. When she meets Peter Devlin, an Englishman staying in the village, it seems that happiness is within her grasp — until she learns the staggering truth about the château and its inhabitants.